CHIVE

CHIVE

Shelley A. Barre

SIMON & SCHUSTER BOOKS FOR YOUNG READERS
Published by Simon & Schuster
New York   London   Toronto   Sydney   Tokyo   Singapore

SIMON & SCHUSTER BOOKS FOR YOUNG READERS
Simon & Schuster Building, Rockefeller Center
1230 Avenue of the Americas
New York, New York 10020
Copyright © 1993 by Shelley A. Barre
All rights reserved including the right of
reproduction in whole or in part in any form.
SIMON & SCHUSTER BOOKS FOR YOUNG READERS
is a trademark of Simon & Schuster.
Designed by David Neuhaus.
Manufactured in the United States of America

10 9 8 7 6 5 4 3 2 1

Library of Congress Cataloging-in-Publication Data
Barre, Shelley A.
Chive / Shelley A. Barre.
       p.   cm.
Summary: Eleven-year-old Chive, homeless because his parents
have lost their farm and are looking for work in the city,
strikes up an unusual friendship with eleven-year-old Terry
and competes with him in a skateboard competition.
[1. Homeless persons—Fiction.   2. Skateboarding—Fiction.]
I. Title.
PZ7.B2743Ch 1993 [Fic]—dc20 93–16202 CIP
ISBN: 0–671–75641–9

For
Billy, Peggy, and Monty

CHIVE

CHIVE

April 8, 1989

"Momma, there's a man coming up our road!" I whipped open the back screen door, letting it slam behind me.

My baby sister, Sarry, started up a noise like a siren from her high chair.

"Chive! You gave us a fright! Now, what is it?" Momma turned from the dough she was kneading on the kitchen table and wiped her hands on her apron.

"A man! There's a man coming up the road, and he's all raggedy-looking!"

Momma cocked her head to the side and went over to the window to see for herself. "Well, you're right about that. He's some sorry sight. Probably looking for a handout." She left the window to go pat Sarry a bit. "It's kind of early in the season to be out riding the rails. Wonder what his story is."

We were the last farm off the highway before you got to the railroad crossing. Fruit pickers and hoboes came by all the time to ask if we could spare some food. I sometimes wondered if the word had got out that Momma was a soft touch.

I squinted through the screen and saw the tip of a rifle barrel slide around the edge of our barn door. "Pop's got his gun out!"

"Well, let him if it makes him more comfortable. I'm still going to feed this traveler."

Momma always called them "travelers," even though Pop said most of them were bums. She liked to say that the pickers were between jobs and the hoboes were between homes, and they were all the same when it came to needing a good meal. She and Pop could never agree about this. The man turned the corner of the house.

"Here he comes!" I hollered.

"Calm down, Chive," said Momma. She pushed some strings of hair behind her ears and picked up Sarry on her way to the screen door. By the time she got there, the man was already standing on the doorstep.

"Morning, ma'am," the man said through the screen, taking off his hat. It was a red trucker cap. At least it used to be red. Now it was kind of rusty with grease marks on the bill. He had on work boots without laces, blue jeans with the knees worn out of them, and a flannel shirt. Over all that he wore a dungaree jacket that looked like it was too small to button in front.

"Hello," said Momma, smiling like he was company she had been expecting. "Can I help you?"

"Well, ma'am—I hope so. I started out this morning from Miller's Creek, and I'm trying to get to Nashua City before sundown. I'm supposed to start working there tomorrow." He twisted his cap around in his hands. "I haven't had anything to eat since yesterday noon and could sure use a bite."

"Why, it'd be no trouble at all. You just wait right there a second. I'll bring you a cup of coffee while I put something together." She turned toward the stove, passing Sarry to me. That was one rule she didn't break. Pop had put his foot down about her letting strangers into the house, so she always made them wait outside.

"There you go," said Momma, coming back with the coffee. The man nodded thanks and sat down on the doorstep to drink it. That's when he looked up through the screen at me.

"This sure is a nice farm you've got here."

"Yep," I mumbled.

"Charles Horton!" Momma said sharply.

"Yes, *sir*."

"Yesssssss," said Sarry.

The man laughed. "You're a lucky boy."

Momma came to the door again, rattling a paper sack. "Well, it's not much. I made you a ham sandwich, and there's an apple in there. And a couple carrot sticks. At least it'll tide you over until morning. Hope they have a hot breakfast where you're going."

She passed the bag out the door, and the man handed her the coffee cup. "My, this is more than enough. I sure do appreciate it." And bowing and backing up, he put his cap back on his head and disappeared around the corner of the house again.

Momma collected Sarry from me, and I ran to the window to watch the man as he walked down our road. He was already taking a big bite out of the sandwich. When he was almost to the highway, I went outside to where Momma was standing on the step with Sarry. She was looking toward the barn, her hand shading her eyes like a visor.

"You can put your firearms up now!" she called.

I saw the gun being lowered from the barn doorway, and Pop stepped into the light. He stood there a second, shaking his head in Momma's direction.

Seeing Pop all of a sudden like that was like looking at myself in the fun-house mirror at the county fair. Everyone said I looked just like him, except for the fact that I was short for my age. He wasn't so tall himself, but he was strong. He had a thinnish sort of face, and if you didn't know him, you'd think he was a very serious person. But Momma knew him well enough, which is why she laughed and waved at him now. Then she put her arm around my shoulders and led me and Sarry back into the house.

"How come you feed those people when Pop doesn't like it?" I asked.

"Because you don't know a man until you've walked a mile in his shoes," she said.

I wrinkled my nose. "Well, I wouldn't want to go *anywhere* in his shoes. They didn't even have laces!"

Momma laughed. "And I hope you never have to. Your father is only looking out for his family. That's his right, and I respect it. But it's not going to stop me none from feeding who I want to feed."

"Chive!" Pop's voice came to us from the yard.

I ran to the screen door. "Yeah?" I called back.

"I think Clover is about ready to calve. You want to come help?"

"Sure!" I yelled and would have been out the door if Momma hadn't collared me.

"Here, take a sandwich to your pop. And one for you." She pushed a plate of sandwiches into my hands and opened the door for me. "Careful!"

I walked toward the barn as fast as I could without spilling the sandwiches and wondered whether the man had finished his in one big gulp or saved some for later.

TERRY

March 24, 1992

Sometimes I wonder what would have happened if I had gone grocery shopping with Mom—if I'd been there to help her with the bags instead of Chive. But then I realize that's dumb because, one, you can't follow your mom around everywhere even if you wanted to and, two, Chive is a pretty persistent guy and, any way you look at it, he would have cornered her eventually.

I had gone out for junior soccer and was coming home after practice so tired I could barely keep my head up over dinner. So, on this particular night I was shoveling it in, not really listening to the usual dinner-table yakking. It's the same every night anyhow. Dad gives a rundown on the joys of advertising with a little commentary on the Loggert Expressway thrown in for color. Mom lets us in on what her jerk boss did and why Old Lou's babysitter is getting paid more than she's worth. And Old Lou keeps blabbering away and dumping food over the side of her high chair for the teddy bear she's dropped on the floor.

Old Lou's name is really Louanne, but I started calling her Old Lou about a year ago, and so far it's stuck. Mostly I call her that because when she's mad, which is a lot of the time, she gets this look on her face you only see on someone who's about eighty. I guess I see it more than most people because I'm the one she's usually mad at. Generally I think I'm a good brother, but let's face it, a two-year-old can get on your nerves.

Anyway, there we were when Mom suddenly pops out with, "The strangest thing happened at the supermarket today." I didn't pay too much attention to this because to her "strange" might be a deformed head of lettuce. "I was just starting to load the grocery bags into the car—and you know it was drizzling this afternoon. . . . By the way, Terry, why did the coach have you practicing in the rain?"

"Mom, like you said—it was only drizzling." I didn't want to hear the sermon again on how soccer was a dangerous sport and what did an assistant principal know about coaching it. "What happened with the grocery bags?"

"Well, I was trying to get the heaviest bag out of the cart—you know, the one with the soda and milk and everything . . ."

Dad and I nodded to keep her going on the same

subject, and Old Lou started banging on her high chair tray with a spoon, going, "Bag, bag, bag."

" . . . and this little boy appeared out of nowhere and said, 'Lady, do you need some help with those groceries?' "

I frowned. "What was he, a Cub Scout or something?"

"Not at all." Mom pressed on. "In fact, he was anything but. He wasn't dressed warmly and looked like he could use a bath. I don't think he was coming from school. But he was very polite— I mean, almost too polite. He kept insisting on helping me with the bags. And, God knows, it was a help. He had them in the trunk in no time."

"Then what?" I asked, waiting for the punch line.

"Yeah, Betty," Dad chimed in. "How much did he take you for?"

"Nothing." She scowled at us. "He 'took me,' as you put it, for nothing."

"I don't get it," I said.

Dad shook his head and chuckled. "Come on, the kid must have had some kind of angle. Selling candy bars for Little League? Bet you bought a whole box."

"Really, Phil, you are so suspicious. I offered him a dollar. . ."

"There, you see?" Dad clapped me on the shoulder and winked.

"Boy, are you easy," I added.

" . . . and he wouldn't take it!" Mom raised her voice to make her point. "Not even a quarter! He said he was glad to be of help and ran off."

That kind of shut us up for a second.

"I don't know," Dad said. "Could be he's from some kind of gang. Maybe he's casing you out, Betts. Taking down your license plate, might have even followed you home." He waggled a fork at her. "Where did you say this happened?" He turned to me. "Terry, you should go shopping with your mother—push the cart for her, do the lifting."

How did I get in the middle of this? "Dad, Mom just told you I was at practice."

Mom passed right over this. "Usual place, the big Food Mart on Briar Ridge Road. Anyway, he didn't look like a gang kid. He was a little boy— maybe Terry's age. It was hard to tell."

I didn't like where this was going. First of all, I was eleven, almost twelve—definitely not a little boy. And now I was getting in trouble because some kid had helped my mom in my place.

"I think he might be homeless or something."

"Nah, too far away from that welfare place where they all hang out," Dad said. "What'd they used to call it? That was a great hotel when I was a kid. I hate to see beautiful old buildings thrown away like that. The Buchanan Arms, that was it. What a waste."

I sighed and went back to my mashed potatoes. I knew what came next—an argument between my parents about "those less fortunate than us." If it wasn't on the news, it was in the paper; and if it wasn't on either of those, it was being debated nightly at my own dinner table.

"Well, Phil, I guess they could heave the poor

people out into the street. That's where they're ending up anyway. And there're more of them every day. Companies are moving out of the area and laying off workers left and right; people lose farms they've had in their families for years. God knows where we're going to put them all."

"Well, I don't think it's our responsibility to put them anywhere." Boy, Dad was revving up for a good one. "These people you're so fired up about are giving this city a black eye."

"How can you say that? They didn't ask to be homeless!" Mom pounded the table with her fist, which was Old Lou's cue to take up the drumroll on her high chair again.

That's when I decided to tune out. They go at this all the time, and when it comes right down to it, I think they enjoy the exercise. Their favorite story is how they fought about politics all during their honeymoon. From what I've heard on the subject of honeymoons, there are better things to do than argue about the state of the world, but if that's how they get their kicks, I'm not going to be the one to knock it.

The argument finally fizzled out over the apple crisp Mom had made for dessert, and we forgot about the kid who slung grocery bags for the fun of it.

"I love appo crips," said Old Lou.

CHIVE

May 12, 1990

"So, this won't be our home anymore," Pop said, and I peeked around his shoulder to see what Momma's face was doing. It had that tight look around the chin that she gets when she is trying to hold something in. She saw me looking at her and pushed Pop aside a little to reach for me. Just in time too because Pop's eyes were getting kind of watery. He turned away and gave her room to slide onto the couch where I'd been sitting ever since Pop had told me to get indoors, he had something important to tell me. On a perfectly good Saturday afternoon too.

"We're going to go stay at my cousin Wade's— in the city," Momma said, rubbing her hand up and down my arm. "You'll like it, Chive. It's a whole lot bigger than Buntsville, with tons of things to do. And you have four second cousins you've never even seen before. Richard's about your age, I think."

I must have made a face.

"Now, come on—this is going to be an adventure. Your pop's going to work at the same tile factory as Uncle Wade, and I'm going to get me the first real job I've had since before you and Sarah were born."

I thought about this for a minute. "Will I go to school there?"

"Sure. You'll go right into the fifth grade, same as you would have here. There'll be more kids, that's all. And—oh, probably lots more after-school activities than you ever dreamed of." Momma, the dreamer. Pop always said she could dream a patch of cucumbers into a shelf a jarred pickles just by looking at them.

Sarry scrambled between Momma's feet and mine, and I bent down to pick her up.

"Hear that, Sarah Jean Horton?" I whispered in her ear. "We're going to live in the city. You better pack up Cow."

"Cow," she said in her baby-bird voice and tried to squirm out of my arms. "Cow," she said again, and I dropped her to her feet and let her run off to find the pull toy Pop had whittled for her when she was born. It was her favorite.

Pop hadn't budged from where he was looking out the window, but his shoulders were twitching. I cleared my throat. "Pop," I said, "I have quite a bit saved up in my bank, you know." I had practiced saying this, and I wanted it to come out sounding like a good idea. "I must have near fifty dollars, I bet."

It was true. I had taken the rubber plug out of the bottom of my tin bank shaped like the First Savings and Loan bank building and poured the quarters and dimes and nickels and pennies out onto the rug in my bedroom. Then I had counted it all up until I got a total of $47.68. I had done it the day Pop and Momma got dressed up in their best clothes and went down to the First Savings and Loan to talk to the bank president.

I had liked the First Savings and Loan ever since the first Friday Pop took me with him to do his weekly banking. It was the oldest building in Buntsville. Pop would push open the big, heavy wooden door and off we'd go, tiptoeing over the thick green carpet, past the marble columns and the mahogany-trimmed walls until we got to the teller's brass-caged window. Whoever it was behind the bars that day always said, "Hi, Earl. How're you doing?" and Pop would chat with them about how much soybeans or corn he'd sold and ask them how their kids were.

When he was done, he'd hand me the deposit slip for safekeeping and two quarters "for your college education." I always thanked him, even though I wasn't sure I wanted to go to college.

Mostly, when I thought about the future at all, I just wanted to stay on the farm with him and Momma and Sarry. But he smiled so wide when he gave them to me, I acted like it was the best idea in the world. Now I thought he might have changed his mind. I had been with him a few Fridays back and heard him trying to make jokes with the teller.

"Yep, that's it. Would have had more, but Ellen turned the last few rows of soybeans into tofu behind my back. No, not really, but if this keeps up, we'll have to live off bread and Ellen's strawberry jam, and you know how tart she makes it." He and the teller laughed, and then there was some whispering. "Yeah, tell Ned I'll have it for him next week or so. I'm going over to High River Market next Tuesday. I hear they're getting good prices."

Every week I watched the number on the deposit slip get smaller until one day I heard Pop tell Momma that Ned Burrell, the bank president, wanted to see them both in his office. When they got home from their meeting, Pop went straight out in his suit jacket and tie and climbed onto the tractor and started to plow the far section of the soy field, and Momma went to bed with a sick headache. That had been two days ago.

Now it was Pop's turn to clear his throat. His back straightened and he turned to face me.

"That's a generous offer, Chive . . ." he said.

But you are only nine years old, and fifty dollars is

nothing, I finished the sentence for him in my mind.

". . . but this doesn't change your future plans. That money's still for your schooling, and I'd appreciate it if you'd keep an eye on it for me. I'll be adding to it again when we get settled." And he underlined it with that little nod of his head that told me we were done talking.

"Can I go tell Jay?" I asked.

"Yes," said Momma and sighed. "I can't think of why not."

I moved to the door, then stopped. "What'll I tell him?"

Pop came over to kneel in front of me. "You tell him . . ." he started, then pressed his lips together like the words were stuck. "You tell him that your pop had to sell the farm. That he couldn't make ends meet any longer as a farmer, and we're all getting ready to move on to a new life. You tell him that, and don't be ashamed of it, you hear? You tell him like you're proud."

I nodded and ran outside.

Good-bye, porch rocker, I thought as I jumped down the stairs.

Good-bye, tree swing, as I hopped on my bike.

Good-bye, driveway. Good-bye, gopher hole. I picked up speed on the dirt drive.

Good-bye, soybeans swishing in the fields. Good-bye, dirt smell. Good-bye buzzing bugs and croaking peepers. I stopped before making the turn onto the main road.

"Good-bye, mailbox," I said out loud, giving the red flag such a hard swat, it broke off its hinges and fell into the weeds below.

So what? I thought and headed on toward Jay's house.

TERRY

March 28, 1992

The next time Mom went grocery shopping, you can bet I was recruited as bodyguard. "Aw, Dad—Al and I are supposed to get together this afternoon to practice ollies."

Allen Drucker is my best friend—has been since the first grade. He and I were trying to get a jump on the skateboarding season. Al wasn't much better at skating than I was, but he wasn't afraid to try a new trick. Sometimes I was, but once I got the hang of it, I could do it perfectly almost every time. Between the two of us we made one great skateboarder. Neither of us had done particularly well at the county skate competition held last summer, and we were determined to make a better showing this year. To tell the truth, I liked skateboarding a lot better than I liked soccer, but I wasn't about to tell Dad that.

"Just go with your mother, okay?" Dad said and gave me his be-a-buddy look. I felt like an idiot going along to protect my mom from some kid she'd probably never see again. Besides, the jerk was so wimpy he didn't even charge for his services. How dangerous could he be?

"I think he's working a different beat today, Mom," I said as we pushed the shopping cart toward the car. I was bending over the cart to drag out the first bag when I heard a kid's voice behind me.

"Hi, lady. How're you doing? Help you with your bags?"

I spun around and tried to look as tall as possible. "Bug off, kid. I'll take care of it." But something must have happened as I zeroed in on the kid's face, because I don't think I looked half as threatening as I wanted to.

"Hi!" said the kid. "Hey, I'm sorry." He grinned. "I didn't know you were with your mom."

At first I thought he was about ten. Mom was right; he was a little guy—at least three or four inches shorter than I was. But something was wrong. His hair was cut in a screwed-up brush cut, not exactly a flattop, which would have been cool, but this short, blondish fuzz all over his head. The skin on his face looked red and dry—like it does when you've been out on the beach for too long. His clothes were weird too. He had on a windbreaker, a nerdy flannel shirt, and jeans that were too short at the ankles. His socks were white and real thin and kind of fell into his sneakers, which had big holes in them. And he talked funny.

"Well, I'll let you folks get on your way." Folks? Sounded like he'd been watching too many *Beverly Hillbillies* reruns. Actually the more I looked at him, the less he looked like he was ten. He might even be my age.

"Thank you anyway. You live around here?" I could see Mom was going to take full advantage of this little meeting.

"No, ma'am." The kid was backing away. "Cool hightops," he added, pointing to my feet. I was about to tell him that my sneakers weren't for sale but stopped before I opened my mouth. He didn't look like a ganger or a thief or anything like that. He just looked like he really dug my sneakers.

"Thanks," I mumbled. "Uh—let's go, Mom."

"What's your name?" asked Mom as I opened the car door for her.

"Chive," he shouted back. Then he gave this funny little wave and ran off—real fast.

"I tell you, Dad," I reported that night over dinner, "the kid's harmless. Weird, but harmless."

"I still think he's from the Buchanan Arms," Mom said. "He wouldn't tell us where he lived, and when I asked him his name, all he said was 'Chive.' "

Dad screwed his face up into a question. "Chive?"

"Yeah," I said, "like the little things in cottage cheese. Some name, huh?"

"Maybe he's from one of those displaced farm families," Mom said.

That would at least explain the "folks" part. "Well, I don't think he'll bother Mom again. I made it pretty clear that his help wasn't needed." Dad gave me a high five. Looked like I was back in good again.

And that, I figured, was the end of it. Except for the fun I was going to have describing this dork in detail to Al, I never expected to even think about the kid again. But I should have known that Mom wasn't about to let it drop. And Chive—he was just getting started!

Sure enough, four days later Mom came in after work, briefcase over one shoulder, Old Lou over the other, bags in both arms, and babbling a mile a minute. "I saw him again! I saw Chive! And you'll never guess what he did!"

"Chive!" Old Lou added.

I couldn't believe this kid had the nerve to bug Mom again after the other day. "Mom, can Al stay for dinner?"

"Did you go to the market again?" Dad looked up from his paper.

She stopped in mid-babble for a second and then rallied. "Well, we were low on milk and bread." Dad's eyebrow went up like he wasn't entirely buying this story. It was interesting to see this look turned on Mom instead of me for a change.

This also gave Al time to ask, "Who's Jive?" I elbowed him in the side.

"Anyhow, there he was! Well, naturally he came right over and was helping me load the bag into the car when I suddenly remembered we needed margarine too."

"Yeah," Dad said slowly and dryly.

"So, I asked Chive if he would go back and get the margarine for me—Louanne was fidgeting and all. And he said he would, and I gave him the money, and he came right back with the margarine—and the change! So, what do you think of that?"

Not much. I myself am not known for running any kind of errand without some form of compensation or at least a little whining. This kid was ruining my reputation. I looked to Dad for some sign of support, but he was ignoring me.

"Huh. Did you ask him where he lived this time?" Great, now Dad was getting into it too.

"Yes," Mom said, thrilled to have an attentive audience, "but he waved vaguely behind him, and I couldn't tell where he was pointing. He was entertaining Louanne—making faces at her and playing peekaboo with the bag. She loved it."

"Chive peekaboo," Louanne agreed.

"And you didn't give him anything?" Dad asked.

"I gave him an apple." Aha! Next time it would be a steak! I knew this kid was in it for something. "I don't think he gets much to eat. He seemed very grateful."

"Mom, can Al stay for dinner?"

"Yes, of course—if I can think of something to fix."

"Well, we know we have margarine," said Dad from behind the paper.

"Who's Jive?" Al asked again as soon as we'd finished eating and were back up in my room.

"Chive," I said. "Like the little things in cottage cheese. We think he comes from the welfare home over on Buchanan Street. He's been following my mom around. You know, like helping her with her groceries and stuff."

"Why would he want to do something like that?" Al isn't much better in the Boy Scout department than I am. He's too busy with his own projects. At the moment he was sanding down the front of his skateboard to make it look like a race car. He's a big believer in the flashier the better.

"Beats me," I said. "I wonder if the kids at that place go to school."

"Probably not. They're always picking up and moving all the time anyway. I don't think any school would take them."

I was glad to hear this. I didn't want to meet anyone like Chive in the halls. He was too friendly, too much of a goody-goody. Besides, he was a hick.

CHIVE

September 18, 1990

"Richie, for pete's sake, play with Charles, will you, please? I swear, you kids are driving me nuts!" Aunt Maureen stood by the kitchen sink, waving a dishcloth like she was chasing flies.

"It's okay," I said quietly from my spot by the little window. I was watching a lady making dinner in the apartment across the way, but she must have seen me, because her arm shot out and she pulled down the shade. I looked up and down and sideways to see if there were any other good windows tonight, but the rest were closed or dark.

"Chive's a baby—I don't wanna play with him. He broke the door on my Rap Monster castle!" Richie yelled.

"I didn't mean to," I whispered, but I didn't turn around to look at him.

"Why don't you both sit at the table and play ticktacktoe," Momma said.

"That's for baaaabies," Richie whined.

"Don't talk to your aunt Ellen like that!" his mother said, and I heard her hand slap against some part of Richie's body.

I turned toward Momma's voice and found her close by in the big armchair. "Where's Pop?" I asked so only she could hear.

She stroked the back of my neck. "He and your uncle Wade went over to an auto garage to look into a job. Remember how good Pop was at keeping that old truck going? He'd make a dandy mechanic."

"I miss the truck," I said.

"No, you don't, you silly." She ran her hand down the front of my face.

But I did miss it. I missed the way it felt to bump along the road when Pop let Sarry and me sit in the back. And the way he'd come up alongside me when I was out riding my bike and give me a lift home. Four months ago we'd come all the way to the city in that truck with our clothes and things stuffed into every corner and piled high over the sides. Then we'd had to sell it when we got here and found out that Uncle Wade didn't have a job for Pop. In fact, he didn't even have a job himself anymore. The tile factory had laid off a lot of people just before we arrived. Uncle Wade was one of them.

"Rrrrrrm! RRRRRRRM!" Richie rode by us on a pretend motorcycle.

Sarry heard it all the way in the bedroom, where she was supposed to be sleeping. "Momma? Mommmmmaaa!"

"Oh, Lord," said Momma. "I hope she doesn't wake the others."

"That's all we need," said Aunt Maureen.

"Maybe she'll nod off again," said Momma, and she scratched some dinner off my cheek with her fingernail. "How was school today, Chive?"

"Fine." I tried to wiggle away from her, but she held me tighter. I could feel her looking at me hard, so I tried again. "They call me things," I said, looking past her ear to the window.

"Like what?" she asked.

"They say, 'Chive, Chive, lives in a beehive,' and they sing 'The Farmer in the Dell.' "

Momma sighed and pulled at the strap of my overalls. "That's because I sent you to school in farmer duds. Wouldn't you be more comfortable in those things of Richie's that Aunt Maureen gave you?"

I shook my head. I hated Richie's clothes. The pants were stiff, and the shirt collars scratched my neck. Even the T-shirts had stupid things written on them like "Born To Be Bad" and "Greetings from Lake of the Ozarks."

"I don't think it's the clothes anyway," I said. "They make fun of the way I read aloud—say I sound funny. Do you know, those kids don't even know how corn is planted? The teacher had to tell them all about how seeds grow and harvesting and everything!"

"I'll bet they don't," she said and laughed, so I did too. "It's only been a little while. Give it time, honey. They'll come around. Hey, how was your letter from Jay?"

"Pretty good," I said. "Mr. Flory is getting a canoe this summer, and he and Jay are going to paddle down the creek to Warmington. He said I could come if I was there. When are we going back for a visit?"

"I don't know, Chive. It depends. Oh, dear, Sarah's still at it."

"Yeah, and she's got Ruthie and Mike up too." Aunt Maureen shook her head and went into the bedroom.

So, it looked like I wouldn't be seeing Jay anytime soon. I knew that "it depends" meant the same thing as "never." It also meant that it probably wasn't a good time to bring up the fifth-grade field trip to the Aquarium. Mrs. Beardsley said we each had to bring in two dollars by the end of the week if we were going to go, and I hadn't even told Momma about it yet.

The apartment door opened, and Uncle Wade and Pop dragged their way in like two cats coming in out of a rainstorm. Pop looked right at Momma and shook his head. Then he smiled at me. "We're getting close," he sang. "Somebody in this big old city is waiting for me to walk in and work for them! I just haven't found them yet."

Aunt Maureen came out of the bedroom carrying both Sarry and Ruthie, with little Mike stumbling and blinking behind her. I put out my arms, and she dumped Sarry in my lap. Then she kept right on going until she got to the front door, opened it, and hollered in a voice so loud it hurt my ears, "John! Come on upstairs now! It's time for bed!" Then she slammed the door. "You, too, Richie. Pick up these toys."

Sarry smudged her hands across her eyes and bumped her head against mine. She was making that little whimpery noise she does when she's tired. I was the only one who didn't mind her when she was fussy like this. She always reminded me of one of the baby lambs, all wobbly and bleating. I knew a lot about lambs and calves and kittens and new-hatched chicks, but Sarry was my first human baby. She couldn't walk or talk or do anything unless someone taught her. From the day Momma brought her home from the hospital, I knew I wanted that someone to be me. Before we came to live at Uncle Wade's, she used to follow me everywhere. Now there were a lot of other people for her to follow.

"I want gum," she said.

Momma turned to stare at her, and I shrugged.

"Where'd she get that?" Momma asked. "Chive,

did you give that child chewing gum? You know better!"

"No!" I couldn't believe she'd think I'd do a thing like that.

"Oh, maybe one of the little ones gave her some," Aunt Maureen said. "Mike steals it out of my purse sometimes."

"How about some apple juice?" I asked Sarry and carried her over to look inside the refrigerator with me.

My cousin John banged into the room, throwing his jacket onto the table and a basketball at me. "Hi, Chivo—what's shakin'?"

I missed the ball, and it bounced off the floor lamp before it rolled under the kitchen table.

"Hey, not in the house!" Uncle Wade yelled at John and me. "And Maureen, don't go screaming down those stairs. I've got the landlord on my neck as it is about having a crowd living in here. Sorry, Earl." He gave Pop a little salute.

"Well, don't you go any further out on a limb than you can crawl back, Wade. We appreciate what you're doing for us."

I poured Sarry a glass of juice and held it for her while I looked around the room. Now that Pop and Uncle Wade were home and the babies were up again, there were people spilling all over the place, looking for space to breathe and stacked up on top of each other like Sarry and me. Even though it was the same thing every morning at breakfast and then again at night, I still couldn't get used to it.

Maybe that was why I liked the window so much. I was glad when Uncle Wade said, "Well, good night all," and we sorted ourselves out until there was just Momma and Pop and Sarry and me left to bed ourselves down in the living room.

After the lights were out and I was tucked into my blanket roll on the rug in front of the armchair, I could hear Momma and Pop whispering over Sarry in the sofa bed.

"I take it you aren't holding back any good news from me," Pop said.

"No, I'm afraid not," Momma said. "The lady at the vegetable stand said she decided to give the job to her niece, who's moving here to live in a few weeks. I didn't believe her, though— especially when she asked if I'd ever used a cash register before, and I said no, but I was sure I could learn. Honestly, do I look too dumb to use a cash register?"

"Wellll . . ."

"Why you . . ." Momma growled.

"Oof," went Pop, like he'd been poked. They giggled and shhhed each other in the dark for a few minutes.

"Really," Momma said, "where do we stand, Earl?"

"Oh, darling, I'd say it's more like we're kneeling. We've gone through almost all the money we made from the sale of the farm. Something's going to have to break for us soon."

"We never should have come here," Momma

said. "It's my fault for dragging us halfway across the state to a place where we don't know anybody or anything. . . ."

"Oh, El, no one's blaming you. We're here now. We'll make a go of it. Remember that summer the beans almost burned up from drought? We survived that, didn't we? Or last year when I broke my leg and was laid up during harvest? Boy, Chive just about brought that whole crop in by himself. Remember? You'd never think a boy that small could get so much work done, would you?"

"Don't know why not," Momma whispered. "He gets it from you. That never-quit attitude."

"Well, you've got to have that when you're his size. Make up for what people try to tell you you're too little to do. He's a good kid. We're lucky that way, El."

"That's for sure. I wish I hadn't jumped on him about Sarah and the gum. It's so hard keeping track of who's doing what around here, I'm turning into an awful mean thing."

"Oh, I think he'll forgive you. He understands more than you think."

"I hope so. We better go to sleep. Sarah's getting all restless again. Sweet dreams."

I lay there in the dark until I could hear Pop snoring softly. The problem was that I didn't understand. Why couldn't we just go home to Buntsville? Pop could get another job besides farming. He knew how to do lots of things. Besides, we had friends there. One of them would give him a job, wouldn't they? Momma could sell her pickles and relishes. Everybody said they were better than store-bought. And I could get a paper route. Or baby-sit—if people would let a ten-year-old stay alone with their kids. I wondered how many jars of pickles you had to sell and newspapers you had to deliver before you had enough money to buy a farm back.

TERRY

April 13, 1992

For the next couple of weeks I was too busy to worry about how my mother was getting her groceries loaded into the car. It was school during the day, soccer in the afternoon, and homework—or skateboarding with Al—at night. Mom didn't say anything about Chive, and Dad and I didn't ask. Until the night I got home extra late from soccer. The coach hadn't liked the way I had bounced the ball off the head of this kid who was in my way, and he made me stay after practice to run laps around the field.

It was almost dark when I finally got out of there, and I rode my board home as fast as I could because I was starving to death. When I got to the downhill stretch leading to our house, I went into a crouch and leaned into a fairly decent turn up my driveway. I skidded under the open garage door, flipped the board up into my hand, and ran in the back door. It sounded like everyone was at the table already, so I threw my gear on the stairs and made tracks to the kitchen sink to wash up.

As I turned to join them, I heard Mom say, "Hurry up, Terry. We have a guest for dinner." I could see that. There, sitting at my place and spooning peas into Old Lou's face, was Chive.

"Hi, how're you doing?" he said before going back to his work with Old Lou. He was really into it too. Now, I personally had never seen Old Lou eat even one pea without a lot of screaming and bowl dumping. But here she was, sucking them up while Chive sang her this dumb song:

> *"The peas grow in the garden,*
> *The peas grow on the hill.*
> *I eat my peas with butter,*
> *I guess I always will."*

I looked at Mom for some kind of clue as to why we had this ratty kid at our dinner table, but she just patted the extra chair next to her and made like I should sit down. Dad wasn't much help either. He was so busy staring at Chive, I wasn't sure he had noticed that I was home.

"Hi, Dad," I said. "Boy, you won't believe what happened at practice this afternoon."

"Sit down, Terry," he said, not even looking at me. "Your mother was telling us how she happened to run into this young man today."

What? He didn't think this was an accident, did
he? This kid had been working on Mom for almost
a month now!

"Chive was helping me with my groceries this
afternoon"—so what else was new?—"and I men-
tioned to him that I was going to be making up a
big batch of chicken tonight, and he said that
chicken was his favorite, so I asked him if he
thought his mother would mind if he came home
for dinner, and he said no, and here he is."

"And this sure is good chicken, ma'am." Chive
stopped his feeding chores long enough to shovel
some food into his own mouth.

Dad cleared his throat. Oh, boy— here it came:
the inquisition. "Well, you certainly have been a
help to Mrs. Caldwell. Do you live near the supermarket?"

"Not too near." Chive smiled at Dad.

"Oh. But you live with your family, I suppose."

"No, sir."

Dad waited for the rest, but I could have told
him to forget it. This kid was a clam. "Well, then—
uh—where are your parents?"

"I'm not really sure," Chive answered politely
and then gave Dad another big smile to back it up.

"I see." Dad smiled back and then looked down
at his plate for a second. "Well, that's an unusual
name you've got there, Chive."

"Yep, I guess it is." Smile. Silence. Chive leaned
over to scratch at something on his leg.

Mom interrupted this fascinating conversation with a little gasping noise. She was looking in the direction of where Chive had been scratching, and she was all freaked out. "Your ankle, Chive. It's bleeding!"

I had to duck under the table to see what she was talking about. It was bleeding all right. From this ugly-looking sore. It didn't look new, like when Al or I fell off our boards or something. There was some tough-looking skin raised up around it, but the center was pretty raw.

"Oh, that's from working in the chive bushes," I heard Chive say above my head. "Had it a long time now."

Chive bushes? My head shot up to see if he was serious, and I was glad to see that Dad looked confused too. "Um, I didn't know chives grew on bushes," he said. I didn't either. I'd seen them in little pots on the kitchen windowsill at my aunt's house, but a whole bush of them?

Chive's smile got bigger. "They do where I come from," he said, and I caught him winking at Mom.

She started laughing, and Dad and I immediately joined in so we wouldn't look entirely stupid. "And where exactly is that?" she asked, wiping tears from her eyes. Much as she liked a good joke, she didn't want to miss an opportunity to get more facts out of our guest.

"Oh, about half the state away from here. Buntsville. Bet you never heard of it. It's real little. Population: seven hundred and fifty. Main product: soybeans—and chives, of course." He laughed. "We've got two churches, one school, the bank, the post office, the general store, and a new ice cream stand." He stopped, and his eyes seemed to get smaller. "At least it was new when I left." His voice got smaller too.

"I crean!" demanded Old Lou.

"And when was that, Chive?" Mom asked. "When did you leave Buntsville?"

"You like ice cream, Louanne?" Chive turned his back to us and faced the high chair. "Hey, you ate all those peas! Maybe you can have some ice cream now."

"I don't think we have any ice cream," Mom said.

"I crean," Old Lou said again, and her face started puckering up. I thought for sure when Chive saw her turn into a screaming little old lady, he'd want no part of her, but instead he got right up and lifted her out of her high chair like he'd been doing it for years.

"Well, I'm sorry now, little lady. It seems we're clean out of ice cream today." Old Lou began to bellow in Chive's ear, but he held fast, bouncing her up and down in a little dance.

"How about a cookie, Louanne?" Mom shouted over the noise.

Old Lou dried up like someone had turned off the faucet. "Gookie?" she asked sweetly. Mom held out an Oreo, and Old Lou grabbed it. She looked at Chive, and they both burst into giggles. She took a bite and offered some to him.

"We probably should get something on that cut, though. At least get it cleaned out."

"Yes, ma'am," Chive mumbled around a mouthful of cookie. "I expect there's a bushel of dirt on these feet. Probably all over me, for that matter." He giggled again.

"Well, you're welcome to take a bath here." She stopped when she saw Dad and me looking at her. "I mean, if you want to. I'm sure they have facilities where you live . . . stay. . . . "

"Why, that'd be real nice. I don't get one—I mean, a really good one—very often nowadays." I'd never seen a kid so excited about a bath before. He handed Old Lou over to Mom and smiled at me. "Nice little sister you've got here."

"Yeah, she's all right."

He followed Mom up to the bathroom, chattering all the way about how he appreciated our hospitality and what a beautiful house we had until I thought I was going to puke.

Soon Dad and I could hear the water running, and Mom came down, shaking her head and smiling to herself. "What a funny kid. He asked if he could use some of Louanne's bubble bath—was so delighted when I said yes."

"Really, Betts," Dad started, "it was very generous of you to invite this boy home for a meal tonight, but I can't say I approve." Mom opened her mouth to protest, but Dad was on a roll. "He seems like a nice enough kid, but we still don't know anything about him, and I think that's the way we should leave it. I mean, how do we know he's not going to be back every night wanting a handout? For that matter, how're you going to get him out of here tonight? We can't afford to get involved in these people's lives. That's what they have welfare agencies for—it's not our concern."

Fifteen minutes later Chive appeared at the top of the stairs. He was all pink and shiny from his scrubbing, but with those scuzzy clothes back on he looked weirder than ever. He skipped down the stairs two at a time, stinking of bubble bath.

"Well, that was real nice." He beamed. "But now I'd better be going." He stuck his hand out first to Dad, who shook it kind of numbly, then to me. I think it was the first time I had ever shaken hands with someone my own age.

"It's very late, Chive," said Mom. "You are going back to the Arms, aren't you? You could stay here, you know." Dad glared at her over Chive's head.

"No, thank you, ma'am. I've got a little sister too." He stooped to pat Old Lou, who was toddling after him. "She'll be expecting me. I've got to be with her." What little sister? And where had he stashed her while he was out chowing down with us? " 'Bye now," he said and zoomed out the front door before Mom had a chance to ask any more questions.

I sprinted up the stairs to my room, kicked off my sneakers, and jumped onto my bed to look out the window. There he was, tearing down the street as if someone were after him. Half the houses were dark already, and he looked out of place running along by himself, that skinny little windbreaker flapping behind him. I wondered if he really was going to that welfare home. I could tell from the feel of the window that it was too cold to be outside all night.

CHIVE

December 6, 1990

"How much longer, Momma?" I shifted on the hard bench for what seemed like the billionth time that afternoon.

"I don't know, darling. Can't you do something with Sarah? Anything! I'm afraid to move from here and miss hearing our name. Take her for another drink of water. Oh, no, better not—then she'll have to pee again, and that ladies' room isn't fit for hogs. She's probably hungry too. Are you hungry, Chive?"

"No, ma'am, I'm fine." It wasn't true, but I knew we'd finished off the jelly sandwiches hours ago, and there was no point in getting Momma all worried about something she couldn't do anything about. I got up and walked across the big waiting room to the row of chairs where Sarry had ended up. She was leaning on the knee of a woman who was talking to her in a language I couldn't understand.

"*Ay, que linda,*" said the woman as I got closer. "Very pretty," she tried in English. I smiled and unwrapped Sarry's fingers from the woman's dress.

"Don't go talking to everybody, Sarry. Stay with Momma and me." Still, it wasn't long before she wandered off again. She walked between two men who were having a loud argument in the middle of the floor.

Momma watched them and sighed. "No one asks to end up like this, Chive," she said. "Some folks just handle it better than others. You've got to keep smiling at people—you remember that, okay? Everybody needs all the smiles they can get."

"End up like this" meant what had happened to us. It meant being on welfare and waiting around all day to talk to a social worker. Momma could never bring herself to say that word—*welfare*—so I tried not to say it either. But I practiced saying it over and over in my head because I figured I'd better get used to the idea.

"Chive, have you finished doing those arithmetic problems your father gave you?"

Doing arithmetic was the last thing on my mind. What I wanted to know was where we were going to stay that night. I didn't want to go back to that last place. They called it a "shelter," but it was more like a garbage dump with walls. Some man had thrown up all over the hall right before we left this morning. And I heard a boy not much bigger than me trying to sell some kind of drugs to a lady. I didn't even like to think about it. Besides, I hadn't been in school for so long, I didn't see that it mattered whether I knew my arithmetic or not.

"No, ma'am," I said.

She must have read my thoughts, because she took my hand and squeezed it hard. "Chive, I want you to keep up with your studies. Please. It's real important to your pop and me. I know our tutoring isn't much, but we're going to get over this bad patch, and then you'll be glad you didn't fall behind."

Out of the corner of my eye I saw Sarry starting to disappear behind some filing cabinets. "I can't watch Sarry and do arithmetic at the same time," I said, trying not to sound too snippy.

"No, I guess not," Momma said. She dropped her hands into her lap and leaned her back against the wall. She looked so tired, I was kind of sorry I'd acted smart.

"Horton?" a voice called out. "Horton!"

"Right here!" Momma stood up and motioned for me to fetch Sarry. The three of us moved behind the counter to a small partitioned-off space that was supposed to be an office. It was stacked high with thick books and different-colored forms, and right in the middle of it sat a pretty black lady wearing a pink blouse and glasses.

"Hi, there, Miss Kellogg," Momma said, herding Sarry and me in front of her toward the desk. "Remember us?"

"Yes, Mrs. Horton. How are you today? Isn't your husband with you? Have a seat, please."

Miss Kellogg was busy shuffling through her papers like she was looking for something. Her glasses kept sliding down her nose, and every other second she had to tap them back up to her forehead. I decided she was about Momma's age, and it came to me that this was the kind of job Momma would be good at—helping people. Momma pointed me toward one chair, and she and Sarry took the other.

"Oh, Mr. Horton's out looking at a job prospect," Momma said. She pushed her mouth into a wide smile, but her eyes still looked tired and scared. "There was a notice on the bulletin board at the shelter that said they were looking for men to haul Christmas trees into the city. I'll bet he must've lugged a ton of trees around our farm. It's right up his alley!" Momma laughed, but Miss Kellogg didn't look up from her paper shuffling.

"Well, that's good. And how about you, Mrs. Horton? Have you found any work yet?"

"Oh, I've been looking, but most of the time I've been trying to find us an apartment. And, of course, I've got the babies to look after."

I wrinkled my nose at her, and she pressed her leg against mine to stop me from saying anything.

But Miss Kellogg saw her do it and smiled right at me.

"Well, Charles doesn't look like he's much of a baby anymore, are you, Charles? By the way, shouldn't you be in school, young man?"

I looked from Miss Kellogg to Momma and back again. "No, ma'am. I mean—yes, ma'am," I whispered.

"We've barely been in one place long enough for me to register him anywhere," Momma blurted. "I've been hoping we'd find someplace soon and get him back in school on a regular basis again. Mr. Horton and I are trying to keep him up with his studies, but you know how that is."

"Surely, Mrs. Horton, you could leave the children at the shelter during the day while you're out looking for work."

"I don't like leaving them alone in those places, Miss Kellogg. They don't strike me as real safe, if you know what I mean."

"I appreciate your feelings, Mrs. Horton, but your first obligation is to find work and housing for your family. The shelters are designed as interim support until you have the means to relocate." Miss Kellogg had put on a voice that sounded like one of those recorded messages. "Now, how has your housing search progressed?"

Momma looked dazed. "Um—not too well so far. I thought we were on the list for one of the Forty-three Parker Street apartments, but when I went there, the superintendent said they were all taken. I waited in line until way after dark, and they didn't even bother to tell us there weren't any left."

"Yes, they went very fast." Miss Kellogg nodded and pulled out a green sheet of paper from the bottom of the heap. "I can put you on the list for Seven twenty-eight Montgomery Place. They have some nice ones for three hundred and seventy-six dollars a month."

"I wanna green paper," said Sarry.

"We can't afford that!" Momma wailed. "Our housing allowance is only two twenty-eight a month."

I pulled Sarry over to me and started playing a quiet game of patty-cake with her.

"Well, we can put you into the Arms over on Buchanan Street. It's forty-five dollars a week, but that would only be for you and the children, with limited visitation privileges for your husband."

"I can't split up my family!"

I left off my game with Sarry and snuck my hand into Momma's lap.

"Those are the rules, Mrs. Horton. Would you like me to register you for the Buchanan Arms or not?"

"No. No, not yet. I'm going to keep looking for a while. But I'd appreciate it if you would keep us in mind for anything that comes up in our price range." She smoothed her skirt and gave me back my hand. "Also, they say our limit is up at that shelter we've been at—on Lexington. Where are we supposed to go now?"

"Let me see." More paper flipping. "I can send you to the one on Tucker Avenue. They might have some room."

"Oh, we've already been there. If you're sending us back, why couldn't we have just stayed there in the first place? Not that I liked it so much. Have you ever seen it inside? They've got men, women, and children all sleeping together in one big room. At least this last one had some screens to change behind. And the food tastes like—well, I don't know what it tastes like. Oh, Lord, I don't mean to complain. It just gets to you after a while."

"You have to understand that we can't give people unlimited use of the shelters." Miss Kellogg was sounding like a record again, and I wanted to know where the switch was to turn her off. "It doesn't encourage people to look for something more permanent."

"Just *being* there encourages me to look for something more permanent!" Momma's laugh was shrill. "Okay, we'll go back to Tucker tonight. If we could have our check now, please, we won't take up any more of your time."

Miss Kellogg looked surprised. "Why, Mrs. Horton, you know your check is distributed through the office that originated your claim. That would be over on Martinique Street."

"But I thought when our records were transferred last month, you said we would be getting our checks here from now on."

"Oh, I couldn't have said that. You always pick up your check in the area of your initial displacement."

"I was kind of depending on having that check today," Momma said.

"Mrs. Horton . . ." Miss Kellogg folded her arms and leaned back in her chair. "I know you have relatives in the area. Can't you rely on them for some assistance?"

"Oh, no." Momma sighed. "We almost got them evicted as it was. Thank you, Miss Kellogg, we'll manage somehow."

Miss Kellogg shook her head. "I wish I had more like you, Mrs. Horton. I get so many who are looking for a free ride that it's a pleasant surprise to meet someone who still has some pride. I truly hope you keep that quality."

"Thank you," Momma said wearily. "My husband and I come from a long line of people who take care of their own, but we're about the end of it." She took Sarry's hand and rose to leave. I stood up alongside of her.

Miss Kellogg started writing something on a note pad. "Why don't you check this building tomorrow? They're scheduled to turn over their apartments to our services in the next week or so, and this will give you a head start. I can't promise anything, but I'll try to call the landlord for you."

"Oh, Miss Kellogg, thank you so much. Where did you say this was?" Momma took the piece of paper and studied it.

"Over past Franklin Avenue, right near the paper-cup factory."

Momma winced. "That's clear on the other side of town from the shelter. It'll take most of my bus money to get there. Not to mention going to pick up the check. Guess that'll mean Earl will have to look after the children tomorrow. I don't mean to sound ungrateful, Miss Kellogg. But sometimes I feel like I'm running around like a chicken with its head cut off and nothing to show for it at the end of the day."

Miss Kellogg nodded, but she had already put our file over to one side and was looking at the next one on her stack. "Good luck," she said.

"Come on, Chive," Momma said when we were outside the welfare office. "We've got to hurry now. We promised to meet Pop in front of the shelter on Lexington. Wait'll he hears we're going back to the Tucker place. And we've got to get something for dinner. I don't think I can eat that stuff they serve there. Maybe we can scare up enough for a can of hash. Oh, I hope your father got a job."

"I hope he brings us home a Christmas tree," I said and grinned to cheer her up.

"Sanna Claus bring me a red ball," Sarry said.

"Christmas! Oh, Lord." Momma groaned.

TERRY

April 14, 1992

"How could a kid live nowhere?" Al asked as he whooshed from one side of the street to the other on his board.

"I don't know," I said, concentrating on getting my board to walk up a curb without dumping me off it. "Mom called up the Buchanan Arms and tried to find out if he lived there, but no luck."

"How come?"

"Come on. How're you supposed to track down a kid with a name like Chive?"

"She could've described him."

"She did, you dork. They've got hundreds of kids going in and out of that place every day. They're all short and dirty and have grungy clothes. They don't care." I realized I sounded a little defensive, and I wasn't sure why.

"Well, I think it sounds cool. He must live on the street. Can you dig it? No parents, no school, do whatever you want." Al bounced up the curb in the same smooth move I'd been trying to get a handle on all afternoon and shook his head. "This is one kid I've got to meet. When's he coming over to your house again?"

"I'm not sure he is." On the other hand, I wasn't sure that he wasn't. Dad had been dead set against Mom bringing Chive home for dinner in the first place, but I had seen something in his eyes when Chive shook his hand good night that told me he might be softening. The way I saw it, Chive was just another one of Mom's charity campaigns. To Al here he was some kind of celebrity. And me— I couldn't decide how I felt about him.

CHIVE

February 11, 1991

". . . So, this fellow said they might be looking for some men to break the picket lines until they get the strike settled." Pop took another spoonful of soup. "But, you know, Ellen, I hate taking food out of another man's mouth. It goes against my grain. Besides, what do I know about plumbing?"

"If you're going to be doing the work, you should be the one getting the money. As for the plumbing part, you fixed my kitchen sink enough times, didn't you? You'll get by. Chive, you're not eating your soup. Anything the matter?"

"No, Momma. Soup's good. It's just that . . . that . . ." It was just that we had been eating pea soup for the last nine days now—I had counted. "I'm not particularly hungry tonight. I had a big breakfast, remember?"

"That's a fib, Charles Horton. All you had for breakfast was a handful of crackers and some milk, and I don't think you had any lunch to speak of."

"Oh, all he needs is a fresh outlook on this old soup," Pop said. He reached behind him for the box of saltines on the counter and pulled out a stack. "You've been missing out on a lot of possibilities here." He plopped a cracker into my soup. "Pea Soup Under a Raft!" He pointed grandly to the cracker floating in my bowl. Then he grabbed two more and crumbled them over the first one. "Pea Soup With Cracker Croutons!" I started to giggle in spite of the look Momma was giving us. "Or"—he added two more crackers to the mess and stirred the whole thing up with my spoon— "Pea Porridge!" Even Momma gave in then, laughing and hitting Pop on the shoulder as he waved my green spoon around in the air. But a barking noise from the other room made us stop.

"Is that Sarah coughing?" Momma frowned and raised herself a little from her chair. The noise came again, and she went running. "Sarah Jean! There, there, baby."

Sarry let fly with another deep one, and I felt it in my own throat. When Momma brought her back, you could barely see her eyes up over the blanket she was wrapped in.

"Earl, fetch me the other blanket off our bed, will you?" Momma sat back down in her chair and propped Sarry on her lap. "Did you see the superintendent? What'd he say?"

Pop brought the blanket and tucked it around Sarry. He bent to kiss her on the forehead, and his lips stayed there for a second. "She's burning up. You still giving her that medicine?" He went back to his place on the other side of the table and pushed his soup bowl to one side. "I talked to the super this afternoon. He said the landlord is still looking into the problem." He said this out of the side of his mouth, like he knew it was a joke.

"Well, we've heard that plenty," Momma said. She was rocking Sarry hard. "We haven't had decent heat for five weeks now. Just that little bit of steam they let up first thing every morning— doesn't heat half a room for an hour! It's not right, Earl. Miss Kellogg says the landlord doesn't even live around here. He's from New York City or something."

Sarry started coughing again. "I ran out of medicine," Momma said. "I tried to get ahold of the doctor at the clinic, but they only have patient hours two days a week and won't give prescriptions out over the phone. Besides, I can't take her out in this cold."

Sarry stopped coughing and said, "Getta Cow, Chive." I slumped down in my chair and looked helplessly at Momma. With all the moving around we'd been doing, Sarry's cow had gotten lost a long while back, but she still talked about it almost every day. Pop had promised to whittle her a new one, but it was hard to find decent carving wood around here.

I reached over to the kitchen counter for a cracker to give her, but the box moved away from me. Pop jumped to his feet. As the box toppled over, a rat hopped out, and Momma screamed. Pop grabbed the broom, but the rat bounced out of reach, spilling soup and clattering the silverware. Finally it leapt onto the floor and scrambled for the back of the radiator. Pop and I tried to corner it, but it was gone. Momma was out in the hallway—still screaming.

"It's okay, Ellen," Pop hollered to her, but she didn't hear him. Sarry was crying now too. I tried to pry her out of Momma's arms, but Momma was having none of it.

By now a whole bunch of neighbors had gathered.

"He beatin' up on her?" I heard one lady ask another.

"Dunno. She bleedin'?"

"Ellen! Please," Pop begged. "It's okay now. It's gone. I promise!"

"I can't!" Momma screamed. "I can't have my babies in there! I can't!"

A boy who looked a little younger than me tapped me on the shoulder. "What's your mom cryin' for?"

My ears were ringing. "Rat," I said. "A rat ran across our table."

One of the ladies heard me. "Oh, honey—is that all?" She started to laugh. "She better get used to

a couple of rats. They've been livin' here longer'n
we have!" She waved her hand at me and left with
her friend.

"See ya," said the boy and followed after them.

Momma wasn't screaming anymore, but she was
still crying awful loud. Pop gently pushed her back
through the door and got her to sit down on the
sofa, and I managed to take Sarry from her.

"I've got her, Momma," I said. Sarry was limp
and heavy. She sniffled in my ear, and I patted her
back to quiet her down. "Sarry Jean,/Where have
you been?/Up and down/and in between," I sang.

"Bean," she whispered. She liked songs. She
sighed a long, rattly breath, and her eyes fluttered
shut.

"I'm going to put her down," I said to Momma.
"She's all worn out from coughing and crying."

"You take her, El," Pop said.

"Oh, my baby," Momma said, taking Sarry from
me and moving toward the bedroom. "My poor,
poor baby."

I was about to follow them, but Pop's hand
pulled me back and led me over to the wall. "Yep,
that's where he came from," Pop said, pointing to
a hole behind the radiator. "I'll have to stuff it up
with steel wool tomorrow morning. Come and help
me clear this table. You and I don't get too much
time alone together anymore, do we?"

I handed Pop the dishes, then pulled a clean dish
towel from the drawer.

"Take care you don't rub the pattern off the plates with that there towel. This is our good china!"

I tried to smile for him, but I didn't much feel like it. We worked without saying anything for a while, Pop looking down into the running water, and me carefully putting the dishes back up in the cupboard, where I hoped they'd be safe from our rat friend.

"Well, I'll tell you, I'm sure glad I nicknamed you Chive, because you've certainly been living up to it."

Pop always said he called me after the chive plant because "they may be little bitty old things, but they sure pack a heck of a wallop."

"Yep, you've been doing more than your share." He winked at me. "I noticed that you did most of the hard scrubbing when we moved in here. That must have been a job, huh?"

You wouldn't have thought I'd done anything at all. The walls were still all different colors from water stains and peeling paint—green and brown and a sickish yellow. The linoleum was gray and sticky underfoot. Momma had put down the good rag rug from our dining room at the farm, but now it was hard to remember the bright pinks and reds and blues she had first woven into it. I couldn't figure out where all the dirt came from. Momma said it was "city dirt"—that it came in through the windows and up through the floorboards, and there was no fighting it back.

All our furniture had been sold at the last yard sale at the farm, with Momma crying over every piece that got carted away. Uncle Wade had given us a card table to eat our meals on—probably because it had one wobbly leg—and three chairs that didn't match. The sofa had come from the street. Pop had brought it home and dragged it upstairs even while Momma was hollering that it smelled of mildew and had a spring sticking up through the upholstery. On the kitchen side of the room, where I was standing, there was a stove and a half-pint refrigerator that came with the apartment. Only one of the burners on the stove worked, and the refrigerator hummed real loud and didn't keep the food cold. The two cupboards behind my head held what was left of Momma's dishes and a few pots and pans.

We were better off than a lot of people in the building because we had a living room *and* a bedroom—if you wanted to call it that. The bedroom was more like a big closet with a small chest of drawers and a double bed where we all slept. When we woke up in the morning, we had to take turns getting up and sliding out between the bed and the dresser. Pop tried to turn it into a game, but it wasn't much fun. It got so most nights I decided it was easier to sleep out on the moldy sofa.

We didn't even have our own bathroom. The one in the hall was for everyone who lived on the floor. It smelled something awful and was usually out of order. I got good at holding it until the last possible minute and then plugging my nose and making a dash for it. The thing I missed most was not having a bathtub. We rinsed off at the sink, but I never felt like I got really clean. It seemed like only yesterday that Momma used to have to nag at me to come in and take a bath. Now I would have given anything to feel that hot water crawling up my chest.

"And you've been going with her to the welfare office and the clinic and Lord knows where all while I've been out looking for one damned job that'll pay a man a living wage!" Pop suddenly threw the sponge—*splat!*—into the sink.

I closed the cupboard door and hung the dish towel over the back of one of the chairs. Pop didn't usually use swear words in front of me. He picked up the sponge again, wrung it out, and tossed it to me, pointing toward the table.

"Your momma's right. This place isn't a fit home for anybody, much less two growing children."

I kept my head down as I ran the sponge over the table surface, rubbing extra hard at any spot that looked like it might be rat tracks.

"I'm going to take that strike-breaking job, Chive," Pop said.

"Yes, sir," I said and tossed the sponge into the sink.

Pop put his arm around my shoulders, and we walked to the sofa. "And you know what that means," he said. He pulled me down beside him, taking care not to land us on the spring.

"Yes, sir," I said again, although I didn't.

"It means that I might not get back here every night. That I might have to be gone for several days at a time. Some of these jobs are out of town, and they don't pay transportation back and forth every day. You stay out there until the job's done."

He ran his fingers through his hair, which was brush cut like mine, then leaned forward and put his hands on my shoulders. "I'm counting on you to look after Momma and Sarah. Your momma's a strong woman, but all this has just about broken her. Chive, you've got a lot of common sense for your age, and you have more kindness in your heart than most kids I've seen—I thank your momma for that. She's going to need all the help you can give her right now. I promise you, we'll come out on the other side of this. But we're going to have to pull together to do it. Understand?"

"Yes, sir."

Pop got up and walked over to the only window in the room. You couldn't see through it, it was so black with dirt and old paint. It didn't even open. He grabbed the iron bars that ran across it and rattled them like he was an animal looking for a way out. Then he turned around to face me again.

"Now," he said in such a soft voice, I almost couldn't hear him, "I'll be needing to see that tin bank of yours."

I nodded and tiptoed into the bedroom. I felt around in the dark for the dresser and opened the bottom drawer, where I kept my things. Holding it tight against my chest so it wouldn't rattle and wake up Momma and Sarry, I brought the First Savings and Loan bank out to Pop.

He weighed it up and down in his hands. "We've got to get Sarah some medicine, Chive. We can't wait for the clinic doctors to see her."

"Yep," I said. Pop was still looking at me all sad and serious, so I added, "That old thing was getting too heavy to carry around anyhow. It's like trying to travel with a bowling ball." I was glad to see a smile spread over his face as he sat down on the floor.

"Want to help me count it?" he asked.

"It's still probably forty-seven something. I haven't put any more in there since we left the farm." I felt my face get hot and red. "Except for the nickel I found under Aunt Maureen's sofa cushion."

Pop laughed and waved me down to the floor with him. "We'll count it anyway. A man should at least know how much he's got before he has to give it away."

I joined him and pulled the rubber stopper from the bottom of the bank. The coins tumbled out onto the linoleum, and our hands set to building them into silver and copper towers.

TERRY

April 20, 1992

The next time Mom went shopping, she brought home more than she'd paid for again. I could hear their voices from my room and leaned out the window to check. Sure enough, Chive was carrying Old Lou piggyback into the house as Mom trailed behind with the bags. I picked up the phone. "Get over here," I whispered as soon as I heard Al say hello. "He's back."

"How're you doing, Terry?" Chive called to me as I came down the stairs. You'd think he was my long-lost cousin or something, the way he was carrying on.

"You staying for dinner?" I asked and caught sight of Mom scowling at me over Chive's head.

He laughed. "Only if I'm invited. I just came along for the ride."

"Of course he is. Chive thinks he can help me with my flowering plum," Mom said. What was he doing now? Applying for a job as gardener?

"Yes, ma'am. I've had quite a bit of experience with fruit growing." Chive nodded.

"Why don't you go out and have a look at it while I put together some dinner. Terry, show Chive where it is."

"Come on," I said without enthusiasm, "this way." Chive squatted down to let Old Lou off his back and followed me out the back door.

It was kind of spooky. As yappy as Chive was with my parents around, he shut right up the minute we were alone together. That was fine with me. "It's over here," I said, pointing to a scrawny tree at the far corner of Mom's flower garden.

"Tsk, tsk, tsk." Chive bent down to examine the dirt around the tree, poking at it with his finger. "Got a garden hose?"

"Yeah," I said, but I didn't volunteer to go get it.

"Well, the first thing it needs is a good soaking. We've got to thaw it out—warm it up for spring." Chive scrunched around on his heels and looked up at me to see if I was going to get the hose.

There's something you can see in a kid's eyes the first time you get a good look at him, one on one, that tells you whether he's all right or out to get you. Al and I call it "the stare," and we use it on everyone we meet. It told us when we met Gary

Samuels that he would try to mess with us every chance he got. And he did. But it also told Al and me when we met each other that we were going to be best friends. Now, looking down at Chive's face, all I saw was a straight-ahead kid. "Where do you live?" I asked him.

He sighed and fiddled with the dirt between his feet. "I can't tell you." He sounded old. Older than my parents, as old as my grandparents maybe. Like he'd seen a lot more of life than he should have and it had taken the kid right out of him.

So that was that. I knew enough not to ask him again. He wouldn't—or couldn't—tell me anyway, and I believed him. "I'll get the hose," I said. But before I took a step, we were treated to Al speeding up the driveway and screeching to a halt in our faces with a beauty of a wheelie stop. Chive almost fell over.

"Hi, Ter!" Al said louder than he had to. "I was just passing by your house and thought I'd see if you were home. Oh, hi! My name's Al Drucker. I don't think we've met."

Chive knew a setup when he saw one and laughed. "Hi, I'm Chive," he said.

"So, what're you guys doing?"

"Watering this tree, dork," I said and started around the corner of the house to get the hose.

Al followed me, buzzing in my ear like a bee. "Well, he looks normal enough. What've you found out?"

"What'd you expect him to look like—E.T.? I haven't found out anything. And get this." I stopped and jammed my finger into Al's chest. "I'm not going to either. We're going to leave him alone."

"You mean, you've got this mystery kid buddying up to your mom and eating dinner at your house, and you're not even curious about who he is or where he comes from or . . . ?"

"Sure, I am. But one, I don't think he's going to tell us, and two, I'm not sure it's any of our business. He'll tell us when he's ready."

"At least you could find out where he got that stupid name. You know, you're talking like he's going to be around forever."

"Who says?" I got down to the job of unwrapping the hose. When we got back around the side of the house, Chive was still standing by the tree. "Well, is the patient going to live?" I asked.

"Oh, sure," he said. "But we'll have to keep an eye on it." So, he *was* going to be around. "I'll show your mom what to do." Maybe.

I went to turn on the hose, but the nozzle slipped in my hand and a spray of water caught Chive. He hopped out of the way, laughed, and took the nozzle away from me. He directed it at the tree for a few seconds, then turned and shot it right toward my feet. It was my turn to jump, then burst out laughing. Chive kept standing there watering the plum tree with this sneaky grin on his face.

"Hey," Al said, "you guys are getting all wet. Why don't I finish the job?" He grabbed the hose from Chive and, backing away, aimed it first at me, then at Chive. Chive and I only had to look at each other to know this meant war. We both took off after Al, chasing him around the yard until we finally cornered him. Then, of course, we wrestled the nozzle out of his hand and drenched him. With all the shouting and laughing we were doing, we didn't even hear Mom calling us from the back door.

"Hey," she yelled. "Hey!"

We stopped and looked at her—real innocent and everything.

"What are you guys doing?"

"Watering your tree for you," I said.

Al snickered behind me.

Chive flashed his most convincing smile.

She shook her head. "Get in here and dry off. It's almost time for dinner. You staying, Al?" She turned and went in without waiting for an answer. Boy, we'd gotten off easy on that one.

With a little pushing and shoving we got the hose propped up and aimed at the tree and ourselves into the house. "Everybody—upstairs and off with those wet clothes. I've left bathrobes on Terry's bed," Mom said as soon as we came dripping through the door. We ran up and did some more horsing around about who was going to wear which robe. I made sure I got my own; Chive put on an old one of mine that was too short for me; and Al got stuck with one of Mom's, which gave us a lot of new material to work with.

"Why, Al, you look as purty as a plum blossom," Chive said.

"Yeah, well, I'd rather be a flower than a vegetable—*Chive*," Al shot back. We started laughing all over again and kept it up until Mom called us down to dinner.

Mom took all our wet things and threw them in the washer while we ate, and that's when I realized why she hadn't been mad at us. It was her way of getting Chive's clothes clean without making him feel bad. Pretty smart, actually.

Dinner was fun that night. Dad made his special spaghetti sauce with the secret ingredient (which I figure must be beer, because I've seen him tip his bottle into the pot between sips), and Old Lou got to sit next to Chive and kick him with her foot through the whole meal. We wolfed everything down, then hung out for a while waiting for our clothes to come out of the dryer. When they did, we changed into them fast, making a big deal about how hot the buttons and zippers were until Mom shooed us outside again. "Don't forget to turn off the hose!" she called after us.

"I'll get it," Chive said.

Al and I automatically grabbed for our boards, which were leaning up against the front steps, and went into a twisting pattern down the driveway, crossing in front of each other every few feet. We were going good when Chive came around the corner of the house and shouted, "Wow—look at that!"

Then Al yelled, "Switch!"

Switch? I had seen guys do this maneuver in tournaments, and it always looked real sharp, but we had never tried it ourselves. This meant that in about two seconds, when Al crossed in front of me, I was supposed to jump off my board onto his and he would jump onto mine. It was too late to think about it—Al swung around my right side, and I jumped in the direction I thought his board should be. And landed on my butt in the driveway with Al's board soloing its way back to the house. Al, of course, had made it onto my board and was still looping his way toward the street.

Chive was laughing his head off, but he came over to help me up. "That was pretty neat, you guys!"

"Yeah, well—not all of us did it right."

Al did his I'm-bad walk back up the driveway while Chive went to get Al's board from where it had skidded onto the lawn.

"These things sure are simple to look at, but they must be mighty hard to ride," Chive said.

I was too busy rubbing my sore spots to answer, but Al said, "Nah, not really. Want to try it?"

Chive kind of shrugged and went to hand Al his board back.

"It's okay," I said, and I took my board from Al

and passed it to Chive. After all, he was my guest. Besides, I wanted him to see how tough skating really was.

Chive turned the board over in his hands a couple of times to get a feel as to which way it should go, then put it down on the ground. After pulling his pants up and his jacket down, he put one foot on the board and started pushing himself down the driveway like he was riding a scooter. Right—anybody could do that. Then before he got to the end of the drive, he pulled his other foot up onto the back, lifted the nose of the board off the ground, and did a perfect kick turn, sliding back to us and neatly hopping off right at our feet. "How was that?"

Al got his voice back first. "Hey, that was great. You really got the hang of that fast. You ever done this before?"

"Nope." Chive leaned down to catch my board as it started to drift away from him. "I used to roller-skate a lot when I was little. That might have helped."

"You've got Rollerblades?" Al asked, impressed.

"Skates," said Chive. "And I don't have them anymore. . . ."

"I don't know anybody that roller-*skates*—unless they're a girl," I said. I was still having a hard time with the fact that the kid holding my board had mastered it faster than I had.

"Oh, no." Chive shook his head. "My momma taught me, but our whole family used to go all the time. At the roller rink next town over. She was real good." Then he shut up like he'd said too much, dropped the board to the ground, and took off down the driveway again. He seemed in a big hurry this time, and I wasn't surprised when he went into his turn too late, spilling himself and the board out onto the street. Al and I rushed over to see if he was hurt.

"Sorry about that," Chive said gruffly. He dragged himself over to the curb and sat down. "Is your board all right?"

"Yeah," I said, checking it out for any scratches or misalignment of the wheels. Then I remembered that Chive might have some scratches of his own. "You okay?" He had already gotten to his feet and was pulling himself together.

"Yep," he nodded. "Just my sneakers," he said, pointing down to a jaggedy rip that had torn his left sneaker from the middle of the side all the way back to the heel. Well, what did he expect for wearing such cheapies? "They were almost shot anyway, I guess."

"Hey, why don't you take my hightops? They look like they might fit you, and I was thinking about getting a new pair anyway." I sat down on the curb and started to take them off my feet. Out of the corner of my eye I could see Al looking at me like I was crazy. He knew how long I'd begged my parents for these sneakers. They were awesome—bright-red canvas, black stars on the sides, double laces, and I had gotten them all broken in so they slouched down at the top. There was no way I could talk them into buying me another pair this soon.

"I'm serious—you can have them." Chive stared down at me, and I banged a sneaker against his leg. "Come on, dork."

He giggled and sat down next to me, dragging off his sneaks and pulling up his skinny socks. He jammed one foot and then the other into my high-tops, then wiggled his toes a few times and smiled. "They're perfect!"

"Are you sure?" I frowned as he started to walk up and down the driveway. "They look a little big. You don't want your feet slipping out of them."

"Hey, don't you worry," Chive said. "I know how to fix that right up." He went flying up the driveway toward the house, with the sneakers making this funny flapping noise on the pavement. "Mrs. Caldwell, ma'am," he called through the back door. "Have you got any old newspapers, please?"

When Mom came to the door, Chive didn't even give her a chance to talk. "Mrs. Caldwell, ma'am, Terry gave me these very nice hightop sneakers, I hope that's all right, because I was skating on the board and fell down and ripped mine up some-thing awful, and so he said I could have these, except they're the tiniest bit too big, but some newspaper in the toes ought to do it if you have some to spare."

He stopped to take a breath, and Mom waved us all in. "Well, I think we can do better than that. Let me look in my rag bag." I was waiting for her to say something to me about giving away good sneakers or at least throw me a look promising a big lecture later, but as I passed her in the doorway, she grabbed my shoulders in a quick hug I had to squirm out of before the other guys saw it. I can never figure her out.

So, Mom got out some old rags and cut them down and folded them into the toes of the hightops until Chive's feet didn't flop around inside them so much. By then it was getting late, and Al said he had to go home.

"Chive, are you sure you wouldn't like to spend the night here with us? Of course, I know you have your little sister to look after. What's her name again? I'm not sure you told us where she's staying?"

"Oh, she's visiting with some friends." Chive, two; Mom, zip. "I think it'd be all right if I stayed over—if that's okay."

It was okay with me, and I knew Mom hoped to find out more about him by keeping him under our roof for a while. "Chive's staying with us tonight," Mom called to Dad in the living room, where he was watching TV with Old Lou.

"Chive!" Old Lou squealed and trotted in to wrap herself around his leg.

Dad came out to the kitchen more slowly,

frowning a little. "Well, that's good. We're glad to have you, Chive. But you boys better hop to it, tomorrow's a school day."

We got to skip baths that night because we'd gotten so wet from our hosing, so Chive and I went up to my room to get into our pajamas. I found a pair that wouldn't be too huge on him, and we talked while we changed. "You lucky stiff, I guess you don't even have to go to school, huh?"

"Nope, I don't," Chive said, but he didn't sound happy about it.

"Boy, I wouldn't mind that." To tell the truth, I couldn't even imagine it. No teachers. No homework. And best of all, no report cards.

"It's okay." Chive shrugged. "I've got other things to do. It's kind of like when we used to get off school during planting or harvest time."

"Oh, yeah?" I was pretty sure he wasn't planting or harvesting anything these days. "What're you growing—chives?" and I gave him a whonk with my pillow.

He laughed and grabbed another pillow. "Yep—working in those chive bushes!" He let me have a good one right in the stomach. The battle was intense until feathers started popping out of the pillows, and Mom yelled up the stairs that it was time to pack it in.

We agreed to a temporary truce, and I was spreading out a sleeping bag next to my bed when Old Lou started up with one of her late-night howling sessions. This usually happened when she had gotten herself overtired or thought someone was still up having more fun than she was—like Chive and me. We went down to her room and found her standing up in her crib, crying her head off because she had thrown all her stuffed animals out onto the floor. But the minute she saw Chive, the tears were ancient history.

"Hi, Chive," she said and held out her arms. He gathered up both her and her bear, and they all sat down in the big easy chair next to the crib.

By this time Mom had come up to see what all the noise was about. She took one look and shook her head. "She got you, Chive."

Chive nodded and asked, "Does she like stories? Can I read to her for a bit?"

Mom sighed and went to the bookshelf to get Old Lou's favorite book about the baby elephant. Old Lou could see it coming from across the room. "Huntoo!" she shrieked. We could never figure out how *elephant* got to be *huntoo*, but that's what she called it.

"Ten minutes," Mom said, "then it's lights out for everyone." She left the room, and I sat down to listen.

"Terry, no." Old Lou pointed a stubby finger at me.

"Okay, okay," I said. I waved to Chive and went back to my room to get my stuff together for the morning.

For the next few minutes we could hear the soft hum of Chive reading in that singsongy voice of his. Old Lou chimed in with the three or four words she remembered, but mostly she just yelled "Hun-too!" every two seconds.

After I got my school gear all packed up and finished brushing my teeth, I noticed that the sounds coming from Old Lou's room had stopped. I tiptoed down the hall to her door and pushed it open. They were dead to the world—Old Lou snoring into her bear's fur and Chive with his mouth hanging open.

"Dad," I whispered down the stairwell, "get up here. I need some help."

Dad came up the stairs, his eyes asking what the problem was, and I signaled for him to follow me. It didn't take him long to size up the situation. He nodded for me to pick up Old Lou, which I did, being careful not to wake her and start the whole routine all over again. And he got Chive, leaning down to the chair and folding him over his shoulder.

"Dump him on my bed," I whispered.

The kid didn't bat an eyelash.

I don't even know what time it was when I sat straight up in my sleeping bag. My heart was banging like a drum, and I was trying to remember the nightmare that had scared me out of a sound sleep. But I couldn't get a fix on it. Then my stomach did a flip-flop when I realized that whatever it was that was spooking me was real and right there in my own bedroom. As my eyes adjusted to the darkness, I thought I saw it move across the front of my desk. At the same time it made this funny little puffing noise.

I remembered Chive was with me and turned to see if he was awake too. But then, of course, I realized it *was* Chive—bumping around in the middle of his own nightmare. I started wiggling out of the sleeping bag to get up and help him, but something made me stop. He was talking in his sleep.

"Run, Sarry! Sarry, where are you? Run!" He moved around the room, patting the walls and stumbling into stuff.

"Chive!" I whispered. "Hey, Chive! Wake up!"

"Come on, Sarry!"

I got up and reached out for his shoulder, trying not to grab it so hard it scared him and made him scream or something.

"Let me go! Sarry?" As he pulled away from me, I got a good look at his face. It was all twisted, like he was in some kind of terrible pain.

I finally caught him and gently shook him until he calmed down. He stood in front of me, breathing hard and blinking his eyes. "Hey, Chive," I said. "You had a bad dream. It's Terry." I led him over to the bed and got him to sit down. "Who's Sarry?" I asked.

"Sarry?" He blinked at me again. "Dog," he said. "She's a dog I used to have. Why?"

"You were calling her. You know, telling her to run and stuff."

"Oh."

"You okay?" I noticed that he was rubbing at his ankle—the one with the sore we had seen that first night.

"Yep. I'm fine." He pulled down the bottom of his pajama leg. "I should have warned you I sometimes sleepwalk like that. Sorry I woke you up." He flashed a smile that looked more like his usual self.

"No problem. I've had some doozies myself. I used to have this one where a dinosaur was chasing me. I was really into prehistoric animals when I was little. So what happened to her?" I slid back into my sleeping bag.

"Who?"

"The dog. Sarry."

"Oh, I don't know," he said, pushing his pillow around until he got it the way he wanted it. "Dogs come and go on a farm. You know how it is."

I thought about that while I waited to drift back to sleep. It seemed to me that if I'd had a dog once, I'd sure be able to remember what happened to it. But maybe he was right about animals on a farm.

The rest of the night was quiet.

The first thing I noticed when my alarm went off the next morning was that Mom was making cinnamon doughnuts downstairs. I could hear the biscuit dough sizzling in the deep fryer and smell the sugared cinnamon as Mom shook the hot doughnuts in a paper bag.

I turned to tell Chive that we were in for a real treat in honor of his visit, but my bed was empty. His clothes were gone from the back of my desk chair, and the door was open a crack.

"Chive?" I called out into the hall. I checked the bathroom and Old Lou's room, then glanced into the guest room on my way to the stairs. The window was wide open. Looking down the side of the house, I could see a dent in the wet grass to the left of the porch. But before that there was the windowsill, a gutter pipe, another sill, and the porch railing. Yeah, I guess it was possible, but I sure had never tried it. Boy, I had a lot to learn from this kid. I went back to my room, dressed slowly, and went down to breakfast.

"You can stop the doughnut factory," I said to Mom. "He's gone."

CHIVE

March 4, 1991

When I first woke up, I thought how nice it was to be warm for a change. I sniffed and could smell Pop burning brush out by the barn. But it seemed closer than that. And different from the other times. Not so sweet as usual. Not like hickory twigs or oak leaves or . . .

"Fire!" I yelled, but my voice came out all squeaky and strangled. As I swung my feet off the sofa, something pulled sharply at my left ankle, and the pain made me sit again. "Momma!" I coughed. My eyes burned, and I couldn't keep them open long enough to find the bedroom doorway. Then, like a gray ghost, she was in front of me.

"Get up!" she commanded.

The doorknob was hot, but it turned easily. Another stinging cloud of smoke pushed me back, and

I bent down to cough again. Having my hand over my mouth and nose seemed to help, and I turned and motioned for Momma to do the same thing, but she shook her head. It was all she could do to hold Sarry and keep her hand over the baby's mouth. She raised her shoulder to her face for some protection, and we went out into the hall.

People were falling through doorways, shouting and crying.

"Mario! Where are you?"

"I have to get my rings! I'm not going without my rings!"

"Close the door!"

"Open the door!"

Most of them were crowding toward the other end of the hall, where there was a large window leading to the fire escape. Momma pushed me ahead of her, and we moved with the others. A man stood on the sill, straining at the window and yelling to the people behind him.

"It's stuck! Get me something to break the glass!"

A woman held up a high-heeled shoe to him, and he looked at her as if she were crazy. "Something heavier! Quick!" But no one turned back to get him anything else, so he started banging at the window with the shoe. More and more people were pushing from behind us, and I felt Momma and Sarry pile up against me.

A big orange tongue of fire curled up from under the bottom of a closed door, and the whole crowd shifted to the right, hopping and screaming. It was getting harder to stay on my feet.

A voice behind us yelled, "Hey, how about the utility stairs? They're concrete! They won't burn!"

Someone closer answered. "You'll never make it! It's four flights down. I want outta here now!"

Some people began heading back toward the stairwell near our apartment.

"Come on, Momma," I said. "Let's take the stairs." I started to squeeze my way out of the crush, looking behind me for Momma and Sarry until I thought we were in the clear. But with folks going in both directions now, we were being bounced around every which way. Then I couldn't see her anymore.

"Momma!" I screamed.

"Keep going!" she called over my shoulder.

By the time we got back to our end of the hall, someone had pried open the heavy metal door that led to the stairs. I slid through the narrow opening and felt people tumble after me. The door closed with a big clank, and we were in the dark. It was hot, but it wasn't as smoky.

"Chive." Momma's voice sounded farther away than it should have been. I tried to stop, but someone pushed me.

"Chive, I can't," came Momma's voice again. She sounded tired, and she was coughing a lot.

I stuck an elbow out and pointed myself toward the wall, where I could flatten myself while people ran past me. I could see Momma's nightgown a couple of steps above me. She was bent over, Sarry dragging from her arms.

"Put Sarry down!" I yelled. "I've got her!"

Momma let Sarry slip through her fingers and tried to straighten up. She swayed a little and started to cough again.

"Come on, Momma! We're already past the third floor."

I tried to lift Sarry, but sick as she was, she was still struggling and crying. I grabbed her hand and bent down to her ear.

"You've got to hold tight to my hand, Sarry— okay? Hold tight! Let's go—I've got you!"

I stayed near the wall so I could feel it and hold on to Sarry at the same time. Every few minutes a big banging noise above us told me that more people were trying the stairs.

"Momma?" I called.

"I'm here," she choked out.

"Come on, Sarry—a couple more stairs! Hurry! It's hot!"

We were rounding the turn for the ground floor when I heard shouts from below.

"Back!"

"Oh, no!"

People stopped suddenly in front of us, and I almost tripped and fell. I pulled Sarry up short by her arm and listened.

"It's all fire! The whole first floor!"

"No, it's not! Come on!"

"Outta the way!"

We couldn't go back. We'd never make it. I saw Pop's face for a second in my mind, and I gave Sarry's arm a tug.

"We're going," I said over my shoulder to Momma, but I wasn't sure she heard me.

Down we went, one step at a time, some people pushing forward and others trying to move back up. I could tell we were getting closer because the heat was getting worse. At last I saw the door to the first floor. It was open, and one by one, people were bracing themselves for the final dash. Some hugged the walls, crying.

Small flames ran up one side of the wall and poked through the floorboards. But someone had made a big jagged hole in the wall at the other end of the hall. And on the other side of it was clear, dark night.

We were about level with the door when a small fat woman panicked and started up the stairs toward us. She was waving her arms every which way, and one swing knocked Sarry's wrist from my hand. I grabbed at the air, other people's clothes, the concrete beside me, but I couldn't find my sister. I had to move forward.

"Run, Sarry!" I shouted and burst through the doorway.

After the dark stairwell I was nearly blinded by the light from the fire. I pumped my arms and kept my knees as high as possible as I sprinted toward the black hole and safety. Pain shot through my ankle again, and I thought for sure the fire had grabbed me, but it only made me run faster.

"Come on, Sarry," I whispered as the hole got bigger and I jumped through to the pavement outside. I kept running for a few more steps, past other runners and men in black coats and people who looked like they thought they were watching a movie until I had curved around the building and found the street curb. Then I stopped and let myself slide down onto the concrete.

I lay there on the sidewalk, listening to my breathing and frowning against the pain that was crawling up my leg. "You okay, Sarry?" I said without raising my head. I held both hands open, waiting to feel the soft plop of her chubby fingers. I sat up. "Sarry?"

I jumped to my feet, and my leg almost buckled under me. Limping, I started back toward the building.

"Momma!"

I went around the corner again and looked into the hole. It was brighter now, the flames swinging from one side to the other. People were still exploding out of the heat, gasping and gulping for air. Behind me they lay on the ground or sat in little shivering bunches. I looked for the pink pattern of Momma's nightgown.

"Momma, where are you? Saarrry!"

They weren't there. They weren't outside at all. They were still inside. My heart thudded into my throat, and I took off toward the hole, ducking a man with a hose and two more people who were struggling to get out.

It was harder now. I had to dodge the flames and keep a lookout for Momma and Sarry at the same time. I tried to call their names, but my throat felt raw and my head was starting to spin. At least my feet had cooled off. I hardly felt them at all as I ran and looked, ran and looked. I thought I saw someone coming toward me who looked like Momma, but a rough hand pushed me away when I reached out for her. I could see the metal door ahead of me and was bending down to knee level, hoping to find something small that might be Sarry, when I was grabbed from behind. I kicked with all my might against a rubber coat, but whoever it was held fast.

Then I found myself out in the clear air again. I was carried under one strong arm over to a red fire truck and set down on my feet.

"Watch this one," the rubber coat said to another man. "He keeps going back in."

But he was wrong. I wasn't going back in again. I was done. I stood there and watched people streaming out of the building and falling to the cool ground. One woman jumped from the second story into a net. A few more were carried out by firemen. But none of them was Sarry or Momma.

I watched the flames and the shooting water and the clouds of gray smoke and the clean people mixing with the sooty people until I felt a hand on my shoulder.

"Chive! Son, are you all right?" Pop squatted down next to me, but I didn't look at him.

"Chive, where's your mother? Where's Sarry?"

Couldn't he tell I was still watching for them? I kept my eyes fixed on the building, checking every window and doorway that might give me a clue. Not many people were coming out anymore, but that didn't mean anything. I had left them in the stairwell. Concrete doesn't burn.

"My lord, what happened to you?" He lifted the bottom of my pajama pant, and I flinched as the cloth brushed my leg.

"Help!" Pop called above my head. "Is there a doctor? Could someone help us?"

One of the black rubber coats appeared at our side. "Hey, this is the kid that ran back in! He yours?"

"Yes," said Pop. "His feet are badly burned, and I don't like the looks of that gash on his ankle. You haven't seen his mother and our baby, have you?"

Of course he hadn't. They weren't out yet. I would have seen them.

"I wish I could tell you," the fireman said. "A lot of people have been taken to the hospital already. Some are probably still piled up at the exits—smoke inhalation. I'm sorry, I don't mean to scare you, but I hate these things. Cleaning up after some lazy landlord. You can get medical attention for your son over there." He pointed to a red and white truck parked in the street.

"Thank you," Pop said and started to lift me off my feet. But I stiffened in his arms, twisting around to keep my eyes on the building.

"What is it?" he asked, but I couldn't stop watching long enough to tell him. Windows. Doors. Fire escapes. Windows. Doors.

I heard him moan. "Oh, Lord, I guess you've answered my question." He scooped me up like a baby, and I turned my head to look at the building as he carried me away.

"Come on, boy, it's all over. You're going to be all right now."

It felt so good being in Pop's arms that for a second I felt my eyes start to close. But I snapped them open again and went on with my search. Windows. Doors. Fire escapes.

"Chive, talk to me, Son," Pop said close to my ear.

Not now. I was busy. I didn't want to be talking when they came out looking for me.

"Chive, please. Can't you talk?" Pop's voice broke and his head fell against mine.

Not now. Not right now.

TERRY

April 30, 1992

Chive had left us hanging. I started to look for him every day when I came home from school, and now, instead of being surprised when he was there, I was sort of disappointed when he wasn't. Old Lou went around chanting "Chive, Chive, Chive" all the time, and Mom continued with her investigation.

When it came right down to it, we didn't know anything more about him than we had before. But you could tell we were all thinking about him a lot. So, of course, I was real happy to see him when he showed up at our front door one night after dinner.

"Hey, Chive." I pulled him into the house, slapping his shoulder and trying to take his windbreaker. "Boy, you missed some great doughnuts the other morning. And by the way"—I lowered my voice—"you've got to show me how you got out that window. That was awesome."

"I've got someone with me, Terry," Chive said. I looked behind him. Out on the porch steps was a little kid with huge dark eyes looking out of a skinny brown face. "This here's P.B. Is it all right if he comes in?"

What was I going to say—no? I opened the door wider but didn't say anything as the kid ducked in the house. I gave Chive a look that I hoped would let him know I thought this was pretty nervy of him, and he answered me by pushing this P.B. kid into the kitchen. "Sit here," he said to him. "I'll be right back."

Mom came out into the hall to see what was up. "Chive! We've been so worried about you. Running off like that the other morning. . . ."

Chive immediately turned on the charm. "Oh, you never need trouble yourself about me, Mrs. Caldwell. I'm always just fine. But I did bring along a friend who could probably use some help." Mom looked around.

"He's in the kitchen. His name's P.B.," I said.

Chive and I followed Mom into the kitchen to inspect our guest. He was sitting where he had been told, hands folded on the table. He flashed a grin at Mom, then looked sideways at Chive. Seems like they all took professional smiling lessons. And, of course, Mom ate it right up.

"Well, it's a pleasure to meet you. So, you're a

friend of Chive's?" Mom held out her hand, which he shook politely.

"Yes, ma'am, I am," he said in a small voice. He reached up and rubbed his right ear.

"Leave it alone," said Chive. P.B. dropped the hand to his lap. "He's been complaining about that ear for a few days now. It doesn't seem to be getting any better either. I'm not sure he's been getting enough sleep, you know?" Or even sleeping in a bed, for that matter, I thought.

Mom was already hustling P.B. up out of the kitchen chair. "Well, that doesn't sound good. Why don't you come upstairs with me, and we'll wash that ear out and have a look—okay, young man? Oh, are you hungry . . . uh, P.B.? We've got some nice turkey left over from dinner."

"Okay," P.B. said.

"I could heat up some mashed potatoes with it— and some corn. How does that sound?"

"Fine."

"Do you have any peanut butter, Mrs. Caldwell?" asked Chive.

"Well, yes. Is that what you like, P.B., peanut but—?" The light went on for both Mom and me at the same time, and we all laughed—even P.B.

"Yeah," Chive said, "P.B.'s mom feeds him more peanut butter than anything else, so that's what he likes best—huh, pal?" P.B. nodded happily.

"Okay," Mom said, "a peanut butter sandwich

it is. But let's take care of your ear first." P.B. looked around Mom to check with Chive and, as soon as he had gotten the nod, bounced off after her.

"Hey, thanks," Chive said when we were alone. "P.B. doesn't have anyone special looking after him. I don't know where his momma is. She has a habit of disappearing."

So do you, I wanted to say but decided against it.

"You know"—Chive's voice went up as he changed the subject—"I've been thinking a lot about skateboarding since the other night. Think it's too late to do some?"

"Nope," I said. "I'll call Al."

Five minutes later the three of us were out rolling up and down the driveway. And Chive was getting good! It was like he had learned some moves just by thinking about them.

"You know," Al said when we stopped for a breather, "you keep this up, you'll have to enter the county tournament."

"What tournament?" Chive asked.

"Every year they hold a skateboarding tournament over at the Morrison Junior High School parking lot. Terry and I entered last year, but we didn't do so hot. But this year . . ."—he paused for effect and to rub his hands together—"this year, I'm ready for them. I haven't been collecting all these bruises for nothing. Besides, I could use that two hundred dollar prize money. Terry and I are going to enter the doubles competition too. A couple years ago these two guys came out and skated to-gether—you know, doing switches and turns around each other and stuff. It really caught on, and now it's part of the tournament."

"Wow!" said Chive. "You mean the best skate-boarder wins two hundred dollars? Lizards, that's a lot of money!"

Lizards? I'd never seen Chive this excited before.

"Yeah," said Al, "but wait—I just got this totally awesome idea." He stretched the words out slowly. "What if we entered as a triple team? It would be a category nobody had ever tried before. We'd have to practice like crazy, but we've got a little over a month. Wouldn't it be wild? What do you say?"

"I say, let's do it," I said. You could see the gears going around in Al's head already. He was trying to think up skating tricks that could be done by three people.

Chive was shaking his head. "I don't know," he said. "I don't even know how to ride yet, and besides, I don't have a board."

"What about your old one, Al? Think we could tape up that crack?" I gave Al an encouraging whack on the back.

"Yeah, he can use it. It should hold up through the tournament at least."

"So, great." I turned back to Chive. "When you come over next time, we'll have it waiting for you." Our eyes met, and I thought to myself, *if* you come

over. If you don't disappear again. Chive looked
like he was struggling with something, but I knew
I couldn't help him with it.

"Okay," he said and let out his breath as if he'd
been holding it for a long time. "Okay, I'll do it."

Al gave a big whoop and stuck his hand, palm
up, into the space in front of the three of us. I
slapped mine on top of his, and Chive's came
down on top of mine. We gave it a good shake so
it'd stick and then got right back to practice.

When it came time to go in, Chive said he had
to get back to his sister, Missy. We asked him why
he never brought her with him, and he mumbled
something about her being sick a lot and having to
stay home. Wherever home was. But he let P.B.
stay when Mom told him that the little guy needed
some good bed rest and medicine for his ear.

Chive went in to say good night to him before
he left, and I overheard them whispering.

"Now, only two nights, P.B. That's the rules.
After that you come on back. I'll tell you what—I'll
meet you halfway—on Thursday morning by the
Army-Navy store. Think you can get that far by
yourself?"

"Yep," said P.B. "If you see Maria, tell her I said
hi."

"Hey!"

"I mean Missy—sorry, Chive."

"That's okay—I'll tell her. You go to sleep now."

Chive walked out into the hall, and I pretended

like I was just coming from my room so he wouldn't think I was spying on him or anything. But then I felt like a dork. After all, it was my house.

"Chive, at least let us drive you," Mom tried one more time.

"No!" Chive said in a louder voice than I'd ever heard come out of him. "No," he said more softly. "Thank you, Mrs. Caldwell. I'll be all right. And thanks again for taking care of P.B. He doesn't eat much—just peanut butter!" We laughed, and he was gone before we could stop him.

Later that night I could hear my parents talking in their bedroom. "It's obvious that he has no home," Mom was saying. "He lives on the street, and so does P.B.—not to mention his little sister. I wonder where he keeps her. Don't you think we should go look for them? He keeps talking about his parents, but . . ."

"No, *you* keep talking about his parents. He doesn't say anything."

"Oh, I can't stand the thought of his being an orphan. He's a wonderful boy—I'd adopt him in a second."

Boy, Mom was getting really carried away. I liked Chive, but I didn't know if I wanted him to be my brother. But, then, I didn't like thinking about his life outside our home either.

"First of all," Dad said, "I'm not sure he'd let you find them—whoever 'they' are. And secondly, he doesn't seem to want to stay with us more than a night here and there. Although you can tell he likes Terry."

"Well, I'm glad of that. You know, it's funny—when they're all outside playing, they're like any other happy pack of boys. But then they stop, and something in Chive seems to shut down. It's almost as if he's afraid to be caught having a good time. My god, Phil—he's just a kid! He deserves to enjoy his childhood."

"I know. But for the moment I think our only way of reaching him is through Terry. All we can do is keep the door open and let him come to us."

Well, it was nice to hear that I was good for something. And I did like the thought of Chive liking me. But I kept remembering what I'd heard him say to P.B. About rules. What rules? And if Chive was going back to be with his sister, why had P.B. said *if* you see Missy? Or was it Maria? I didn't get it. I wasn't even sure I wanted to get it. All that was important was that he'd have to come back now. We were a team!

CHIVE

June 7, 1991

"Keep away from my son, you hear?" Pop yelled. "I mean it! If you touch my boy again, I'll kill you with my bare hands! I swear I will!" Pop struggled against the security guard who was holding on to him while the old man stood there, smiling around the gap in his crummy teeth. "You call this a shelter? What kind of shelter is this for a young boy if he's going to be pawed at by something like that?"

"Come on, now, mack, let's settle down," the guard grunted into the back of Pop's head. He got ahold of both Pop's arms and yanked them up behind him so hard, Pop had to stand on tiptoe to keep his shoulders from being pulled out of the sockets.

The shaking started to crawl up my back again, so I pushed my spine into the corner and let myself slide down the wall until I was sitting on the cold tiles. I tried to angle my head so I didn't have to look into the old man's face. I could still feel the grease on my hands from when I'd pushed him off me. And the smell. It was a mixture of sweat and bad food, and thinking about it made me feel like I was going to throw up again. Maybe it was me I smelled.

Because I had thrown up. As soon as I woke up and realized that old buzzard's hand was rubbing across my stomach—as soon as I opened my eyes and saw his stubbly chin resting on the pillow next to my face, I had pushed him away with all my strength, and then I had thrown up. The guard must have heard me, because next thing I knew, there was a flashlight shining in my eyes.

"No trouble here," the old man had said sweetly, removing his hand from my stomach and draping it across my shoulders.

I didn't care what the guard did to me—I bolted. I went running through the dark, bumping into beds and tripping over clothes that had been thrown onto the floor, with the guard and the buzzard right behind me.

"Hey, kid! You better stop if you know what's good for you!" The guard was gaining on me.

"Come back here, little fella! I didn't mean nothin' !"

And we were starting to wake people up.

"Hey, man!"

"What is this?"

"People are tryin' to sleep!"

On my third pass around the room I saw a familiar shadow out of the corner of my eye. That was when everybody stopped chasing me, and the fight between Pop and the guard started up in the middle of the room.

Now Pop twisted around in the guard's grip. He was looking for me. "Where is he? Chive?"

I opened and closed my mouth a few times and heard my teeth chatter. As soon as Pop saw that I was sitting safely behind him, he relaxed, and the guard let him go.

"Are you all right?" Pop came over and felt of my arms and legs, like maybe I had broken something. "What did he do to you, huh, boy? Did he hurt you?"

The old man let out a high, wheezing giggle from behind the guard. "Hurt him? Why would I want to hurt him? Nice little boy like that. I was just tuckin' him in." And he giggled again until it made him cough.

Pop stopped patting me, and his eyes blazed red. He pivoted away from me, still in a squat, and looked like he would have pounced if the guard hadn't grabbed the old man by the sleeve.

"You, too, gramps. That's enough for tonight. Can't you leave the little ones alone? One more time and you're out of here, pal. I think you better come with me, where I can keep an eye on you." The guard led the old man out the door of the sleeping room, and I could hear him giggling and wheezing all the way down the hall.

"Let's go, Son." Pop hauled me to my feet.

We went back to where I had been sleeping, and Pop ran his hand around under the cot until he found the plastic bag we kept our things in.

"You got everything here?" he asked, looking into the bag. "Socks, T-shirts, hairbrush . . . Where's your toothbrush?"

I took my toothbrush from the milk crate beside the cot and dropped it into the bag.

Pop nodded. "And your sweater. Where's your sweater?"

I stared at Pop's questioning face. I had been sleeping on my sweater. I had rolled it up like a pillow and put it under my head. Frantically I dug through the dirty bed sheets.

"Come on," Pop said, taking my arm and pulling me out into the hallway. "Hey!" he yelled down to the end, where he could see the guard sitting at a desk with the old man propped up on a bench beside him. "Hey, that man took my boy's sweater!"

The guard frowned at Pop. "Now what is it?"

"I'm asking you to check that man for my son's sweater."

Pop held me tightly by the arm while the guard shook his head and leaned over to the buzzard.

"I didn't steal nothin'," the old man whined and leaned away.

"Come here before I make you come here," the guard growled, and the old man opened his arms in surrender. The guard pulled at the man's grubby overcoat, patting him for lumps and digging his hands into the deep pockets. "Nothing."

"Well, he must have hidden it somewhere. Maybe in his cot?" Pop looked back down the hall and shook his head. "Never mind," he said. "Let's get out of here, Chive."

We were walking past the shelter reception desk when a voice stopped us.

"Excuse me," the lady called. "Where are you taking that boy?"

Pop turned and kept a hand on my shoulder. "He's my son. I'm taking him with me."

"Oh, you can't do that." The lady came out from behind the desk. "Why, it's the middle of the night. Besides, if you withdraw him now, I can't guarantee we'll have a space for him tomorrow night. Have you been staying here with him? I don't remember seeing you before. Isn't this boy the deaf-mute?"

"Ma'am," Pop said as he drew me behind him and started edging toward the door, "if I haven't been here with my son, it's because I've been out trying to scare up enough money to get him out of places like this. And you don't have to worry about saving him a space for tomorrow night because he won't be coming back. And he's not a deaf-mute. He just doesn't have anything to say to the likes of you!" We had reached the door, and Pop pushed me aside and swung it open.

"Sir, this will be reported to the welfare office! You are depriving your son of his rights! Guard!" she called as the door slammed behind us.

We took off running down the street, with Pop laughing and hooting like crazy. "Whooooeeee! Guess I sprung you from that place! Hey, boy—let me read you your rights!"

When we finally stopped running, Pop was still laughing. He leaned up against a lamppost and gasped and laughed and gasped some more. I was trying to laugh along with him until I realized he wasn't laughing anymore.

He turned in toward the post and leaned his eyes into his arm. His shoulders shook, and he sounded like he was swallowing air. He pulled away from the lamppost and hauled off and gave it a kick. Then another kick. Then he started beating at it with his fists until I stuck my hand out and grabbed him by the back of his shirt. When he felt me tugging at him, he slowed down and dragged his sleeve across his eyes. His breathing quieted some, and he looked down at me.

"I'm sorry," he said.

I gave him a half smile and thought this might be a good time to start talking to him again. But no words came. I could never think of anything to say anymore. Nothing except that I was sorry, too, but I didn't think that's what he wanted to hear. I picked up our plastic bag and waited.

"Okay," he said, giving his eyes one more swipe. "I think they still might be serving coffee and soup over on Tucker Avenue. I could use a little soup. How about you?"

We started out at an easy pace.

"Oh, yeah—and I want you to have this." He dug in his pocket and slapped something into my hand. I knew without looking at it what it was. I brought it up to my eyes anyway, and the street-lights picked up its silver edges. Pop's pocket knife. The one with all the different-sized blades that had opened soda bottles, sliced apples, whittled toys for Sarry and me—this knife could do anything.

"Remember how I taught you to flip it open?" he asked.

I nodded and positioned it just so in my hand. A flick of my wrist and the knife clattered to the sidewalk. I hurried to pick it up.

"That's okay. You'll get the hang of it. Besides, it's not a toy." He stopped walking and turned to face me. "This is all the protection I've got to give you right now. It's not much, but until things get better for us, you're going to be on your own a lot." He turned back toward the street and motioned with his head for me to follow him. "You see this, Chive?"

I looked ahead, and as far as I could see, there was nothing but rows of broken buildings and bits of garbage flying around in the wind. Something moved out of the shadows a block away, and a man in a fancy hat crossed the street. Close by, a car alarm went off, making me jump a little.

"This is where we live now. I'm not going to

leave you alone in those shelters again, you can be sure of that. I can't even afford to put you up in that Buchanan Arms—not that I'd want to anyway. No, I think we'll take our chances right out here on the street. We're going to have to make the best of it, Chive."

I put my hand around the back of his waist because I thought he needed it. And he put his arm around my shoulders. And we went to get some soup.

TERRY

May 12, 1992

During the next couple of weeks we saw Chive a lot. Sometimes he'd even be waiting for me on the front porch, my board in one hand and some cookies Mom had given him for us in the other. We'd hit the concrete right away—him, Al, and me—practice until dinner, and then come back out for more. It was great because the days were getting longer, and it got dark later and later. It was all Mom could do to drag us into the house at night.

This was serious stuff we were doing. Al had added some fancy footwork to his solo program, and I knew he had his eye on first prize. "Think anyone else will be doing a kick flip?" he asked us. "How about an air walk?"

Meanwhile Chive was skating as if he'd been born on a board. It was almost weird. He'd look at something Al did and then repeat it right after him. Al didn't like it too much either. "Hey, veggie," he said. "Get your own routine."

Chive just laughed and started working on something else. But he was definitely a contender. He'd try anything.

Hanging out with these two stars, it didn't take me long to figure out that I wouldn't be going for any big prize money, so it was decided that I would be in charge of the team material. And, boy, were we hot! We had the three-man switch down to a science, and we were practicing a moving braid and a leapfrog.

Most of the time Chive brought P.B., who liked nothing better than to sit on the porch, giving un-asked-for criticism like "That looked pretty lame" or "Why don't you try a three-man crack the whip? That'd be neat!"

"That would also make us dead!" Al said.

"Really?" P.B. asked before going back to his play-by-play.

Sometimes he even showed up by himself. Mom always took him right in, gave him his peanut but-ter sandwich, and put him to bed early if he looked tired. Any questions we had about Chive's where-abouts went unanswered. I wondered if this was part of the "rules" I'd heard them talking about. If so, P.B. was good at keeping them.

As the day of the tournament got closer, it was obvious that Al's old board wasn't going to make it. The tape was starting to give out, and every time Chive came down too hard on it, the board would bend. Then I got this great idea.

"Dad, can I have an advance on my allowance? I'll pay it back with lawn mowing." This was a surefire winner. Dad hated mowing the lawn and had an even harder time trying to get me to do it.

"Hmmm, I'll think about it. What do you need an advance for?"

"My birthday's coming up, right?"

"Right."

"Well, Chive doesn't have his own skateboard for the tournament. So, I thought maybe I could get him one and give it to him on my birthday, since we don't know when his birthday is, and this way it wouldn't embarrass him so much because it would be all one big party sort of thing."

Dad got it right away. He looked like he was doing some figuring for a second and then dug into his pocket. "I'll tell you what," he said, pulling out some bills. "I'll give you the advance for Chive's board now, and you can pay me back half. How would that be?"

"That'd be great. Thanks, Dad. Does this mean I only have to mow half the lawn?" He gave me a swat on the butt, and I ran upstairs to look in the catalog for a good board.

CHIVE

August 14, 1991

I liked the supermarket. Of all the places within walking distance of where Pop and I hung out, this was my favorite. It was pretty far too—fifteen blocks, I'd counted. But it was worth it. I didn't come here for the food. Pop and I usually did our shopping at the all-night delicatessen behind the Buchanan Arms, where we could get canned goods cheap or cheese and meat ends they were going to throw out anyway. When you got right down to it, it was really the supermarket parking lot I liked. It was so—normal. It reminded me of the big grocery store we used to go to in the next town over from Buntsville. I liked to watch the people.

Today had been a hot one, but now the sun was starting to bend, and the folks pulling in after work didn't look so melted. I leaned up against the cool brick beside the door and played my usual game of trying to guess about the lives of the people going in and out of the store. Like this lady here. She was hurrying along like a mouse—even with the heat. She didn't look left or right, just headed for the door. Probably lived alone—coming in to get a little something for her dinner. A car door slammed, and a boy about sixteen and his girl-friend came toward the store, clutching at each other and smooching.

As they got to the "in" door, the "out" door next to me swung open, and a lady pushing a full cart of bags came charging out. Her hair was twisted into a long braid that hung down her back, and she was wearing cut-off jeans with a short sleeved shirt. Her purse banged against her hip as she tried to point the cart in the direction of her car. She was navigating a turn to line the cart up beside her trunk when she hit a bump in the pavement. A roll of paper towels that had been sticking out of one of the bags bounced over the side. A box of crackers was about to follow it.

"Yipes!" she squealed as the rest of the bags started to topple.

I didn't even think. I ran toward the cart.

"Got 'em!" I heard myself say, and my chest caught the bags before they spilled to the ground.

"Wow!" said the woman. "That was close!"

I cleared my throat and bent down to pick up the paper towels and a couple of cans that had escaped. I had scared myself by talking right out loud like that, and I wasn't sure I could do it again.

"You really saved me there!" The lady took off her sunglasses and put them on top of her head, and right away I thought of Momma. Same soft green eyes. Same smile. Maybe that's why I'd run to help her. I could tell she was waiting for me to say something, so I shrugged and nodded. And smiled back.

"Well, I guess I'd better get these things in the car before they get away from me again," she said and put her key in the lock of the car trunk.

I pulled one of the bags out of the cart and went to stand beside her.

"Well, thank you," she said as I lifted the bag through the open hatch.

I felt my face growing red, so I turned around to get another bag. In a couple of minutes I had all the groceries arranged snugly in the trunk. I stepped back and put my hands in my jeans pockets.

She started fishing around in her purse, so I figured she didn't need me anymore. I was a few steps away when I heard her call me.

"Oh, wait a minute! Here—please, take this. Thanks for your help." She smiled that smile again and stuck her hand out.

I looked into it and saw two quarters. It surprised me, and I started shaking my head. "Oh, no, ma'am," I mumbled, backing away.

"Oh, please," she said, walking toward me with the money. "Really—you were a big help."

"That's okay," I managed to get out. "You keep it."

That made her stop, and I saw her face change. I stopped, too, and tried to tuck my T-shirt into my jeans. I remembered that Pop and I hadn't been to one of the shelters for a sponge bath in about a week. And my hair needed cutting again, and this T-shirt had a rip in the shoulder. Sometimes I forgot that I didn't look like other kids—kids who'd gotten up that morning, taken a shower, and put on the clean clothes their mommas had left neatly folded for them in their dresser drawers.

But I didn't want her looking at me that way anymore, so I gave her a big smile. " 'Bye, lady," I said, a little more sure of my voice, and turned to go.

"Hey!" she called again.

I looked over my shoulder.

"At least take these!" She was holding out the box of crackers.

My stomach growled, reminding me that I hadn't had anything to eat since the can of beans I had finished off the night before.

"Come on," she said, teasing. "Working boys have to keep up their strength."

I felt my face go red again, and I walked back toward her.

"Thanks again," she said, shoving the box into

my hands and slamming the trunk door. "You take care, now." She tipped the sunglasses down onto her nose again and got in the car.

"Yes, ma'am!" I called and waved as she drove out of the parking lot. I headed for the side of the supermarket and the street that would take me back to where Pop and I were living for the week.

"Ritz," I read aloud to myself as I walked. I remembered this kind of crackers. Momma used to put squiggly cheese on them when we had company. I could eat some for dinner tonight and a few more for breakfast tomorrow morning, and then maybe I'd save some for when Pop got back. Of course, that wouldn't be until the weekend, and this was only Wednesday—a long time to keep a full box of crackers hanging around. I was trying to remember what kind of job Pop had said he was going to be on when something hit me from the side.

I jumped away, holding the box up over my head in case it was a dog. But it wasn't. It was a kid. A little black kid dressed in a tank top, shorts, and rubber sandals.

"Sorry!" he said. "I'm in a hurry."

I frowned at him, still holding my crackers out of reach. And wrinkled my nose when I got a whiff of him. Peeeyew! His hair had bits of gray dirt tangled in the tight curls, and he was trying to haul up the waistband of his shorts and scratch a scab on his elbow both at the same time.

"Hey, whatcha got?"

I wrapped my arms more tightly around the cracker box and started to pass him.

"What's your name? My name's Dwight. I was named after an old President. Where're you going?" Now he was following me, which I didn't like at all. "I'm going over to the diner. They throw out their garbage about this time every day, and you can get some really good stuff. I found a piece of ham last night, and there's always bread—you just have to pick off the blue spots. Do you live at the Arms? We did for a while, but we got thrown out for cooking on a hot plate."

I tried to walk faster, but he stuck to me like glue. Couldn't he tell that I couldn't talk? Or, at least, that I wasn't going to talk to him? I had seen kids like him in the food lines—hanging all over their folks, crying and picking fights with each other. Their mommas had to keep screaming at them to stay in line and behave. I didn't like them. I *wasn't* like them. I would *never* be like them. I started walking faster, and he did a little hop to keep up with me.

"You've got to be careful, though. I ate a burger from the diner once, and it made me sick. Of course, if you give me some of your crackers, I won't have to go. How about two? Or three?" He held up three fingers in front of a hopeful smile.

"No!" I shouted into his face. I scared him enough that he stopped dead in his tracks, and it gave me a chance to put some distance between us. I broke into a run.

"Okay!" he yelled after me. "Maybe next time!"

There wasn't going to be a next time. Any food I could get was for me and Pop. Maybe I'd go back to the parking lot tomorrow. Maybe that lady would be there again. No, that was silly—she wouldn't come two days in a row. But maybe there would be someone else like her. I thought of what Momma used to say—about how folks will give a lot in exchange for some nice talk and a helping hand. Maybe they'd give me something to eat. If they did, I sure wasn't going to share it with any scruffy kid. Anyway, what was a kid like that doing out on the street, picking through garbage by himself? He couldn't be more than six, seven. And if he didn't live at the Arms, where did he live?

I slowed down. My run had made me hungrier, so I opened the box. I pulled one round cracker from the waxed-paper lining and popped it into my mouth. The warm taste of butter and salt almost made my eyes water. Without thinking I took out two more and stuffed them in, too, one on top of the other. Boy, it was hard to stop once you got started with these things.

I peered into the box and decided there were plenty left for later. And enough for Pop if I stopped now. I looked behind me at the four blocks I had run. The kid was nowhere in sight. Probably on his way to that diner.

I stood there a minute more before I closed up the box and started trotting back over the same blocks, looking left and right as I crossed each in-tersection. No kid there. Not there either. I was almost all the way back to the supermarket when I saw him down a side street. He had a trash-can lid in one hand and was digging into the can with the other.

"Hey!" I called to him. He jumped, like he wasn't sure what I was going to do to him. "I thought you were going to the diner."

"Yeah, I was," he said, looking down into the can. "But sometimes you can do just as good in this neighborhood."

I didn't have to look around me to know what he meant. Every time I walked to the supermarket, I passed these streets. This was where people with money lived. They had nice lawns and white- or blue-painted houses with basketball hoops nailed over the garage doors. New cars sat in the drive-ways, and sometimes you'd see the folks them-selves, rushing in and out of their front doors or sitting on their porches with something cool to drink.

"These people eat a lot of frozen food," Dwight said. "But they must not like it, because they're always throwing part of it away. See, here's some spaghetti-looking stuff!"

Dwight was starting to lift a tomato-y cardboard container out of the can when I saw the front door of the house open. A man leaned out, waving a rolled-up newspaper and yelling, "Hey, you kids!

Get out of there! I mean it! Get away from here or I'll call the cops!"

I grabbed Dwight's hand, loosening the container from his fingers, and dragged him down the street as fast as I could. We didn't stop running until we hit Carter Street. I sat down on the curb, but Dwight stayed standing with his hands on his hips.

"Phooey," he said. "That looked really good. I hate when that happens."

The sun had sunk lower in the sky, and I had to squint to look up at him. "You do this a lot?"

"Uh-huh. But mostly I don't get caught." He giggled and sat down next to me.

If he was as hard up as he looked, I couldn't figure out what he had to laugh about. "So, where do you live, Dwight?"

He put his chin on his hands and his elbows on his knees and settled in for a friendly chat. "Oh, different places. Linda finds friends for me, and I stay with them for a while. Or she and I sometimes sleep at the shelter on Lexington."

I shuddered at the mention of that shelter, and Dwight looked worried for a second. I tried to laugh it off and said, "Yeah, I know the place. Gives me the creeps."

Dwight stuck his tongue out in agreement, and we laughed together. "The only thing I like about it is when Maria is there. She's my best friend even though she's a girl," he said. "Her mom's nice, too, but she has to leave Maria alone a lot while she looks for an apartment, so Linda and I keep an eye on her."

"Who's Linda? Here—have a cracker." I opened the box, and Dwight dove right in, coming up with about five crackers in his fist.

"Thanks," he said and began munching noisily. "Linda's my mother, but she doesn't like me to call her Mom. She's real pretty and has a lot of boyfriends."

"Where is she now?"

Dwight shrugged and looked hungrily at the cracker box again. I passed it to him. "I'm not sure. She had to do something with Jimmy. He's her new boyfriend, and she says he has a lot of money and an apartment. She told me to meet her on the steps of the Catholic church on Thursday after the church bells ring." His face scrunched up. "Is this Thursday?"

"No," I said. "It's only Wednesday."

He grinned and helped himself to another cracker.

"So, where're you going to sleep tonight?" I asked him.

"Probably with Buddy. He sleeps under the stairs of the burned-out building on Maple, and he lets me stay with him—if he isn't doing business."

"What kind of business is Buddy in?"

"I don't know, but a lot of important people come to visit him. This one man has a *long* fur coat that he wears even in summer!"

I sighed and stood up. "Hey, how'd you like to

spend the night with me? Pop and I are staying in an abandoned brownstone right around here. It's not too clean, but the cops don't bother us."

Dwight jumped up beside me. "Really? Is Pop your dad? Wow, that's cool!"

"Yep, he's my dad. But he's off working on a job right now. I don't expect him back until Saturday—maybe Sunday."

"Oh." He sounded disappointed.

"Maybe you could come back then and meet him. If it's okay with your momma—I mean, Linda."

"Yeah! That'd be a good idea. Or I could just wait for him with you. Sometimes Linda doesn't make it, so I might be free for the rest of the week. Hey, maybe Maria could come too! We could leave a note for her mom. So, you think he'll really be back on Sunday?"

"Who, Pop? Yeah, he'll be back. He always comes back. Think we should save him some of those crackers?"

"Yeah," said Dwight, giving up the box and offering me a crumb-covered hand to hold.

We walked along for a bit without saying anything. The evening was finally turning cool, and it was nice to have someone to walk with, but my head was spinning. First there'd been the lady at the market, and now I was inviting a kid back to Pop's and my hiding place. Maybe two kids! I hoped Pop wouldn't be mad. But how could he be?

He'd never let a kid stay out alone on the street like that. Well, of course, I was alone a lot myself—but that was different. I was almost eleven, and these kids were just—just little. Boy, if I was going to have visitors for the next few days, I was going to have to get my hands on more food. Maybe another pass at the supermarket tomorrow—you could never tell.

"We almost there?" Dwight asked. His hand felt heavier in mine, and I noticed that his eyes were beginning to droop.

"Yep. Let's stop at the deli first and see if we can get some baloney. The man there knows me, and he might give me some of the stringy parts. People don't like that on their sandwiches."

"Okay," Dwight said. "You think he's got any extra peanut butter he doesn't want?"

"Peanut butter? I don't think so. Why?"

"No reason." We walked on a little more. "I like peanut butter," Dwight whispered. "That's what Linda makes—peanut butter sandwiches."

"We'll see if we can scare some up." I squeezed his hand, and he answered with a little skip.

TERRY

May 29, 1992

My birthday landed on a Friday this year, which meant we could go all out for my party without worrying about school the next day. Al was there, of course, and Chive and P.B. came together.

We were all talking skateboarding when P.B. asked, "How old are you, Terry?"

"Twelve and too old to be hanging out with a bunch of babies like you!"

"Yeah, right," said Al. "As if two months' difference makes you Mr. Maturity." I loved giving Al grief about me being older than him during the only time of the year that I could. In August we'd be celebrating his birthday, and the score would be evened up again.

We had hot dogs and burgers that Dad cooked on the grill, and then it was time for dessert. Mom lit the candles and carried my cake in with Old Lou leading the singing. Everyone reminded me to make a wish, but I had trouble deciding on just one. So I made two. The first was that our triple team would clean up at the tournament. And the second was that Chive would let me in on his secret life. Then I blew my brains out until all the candles were dead and there was quite a bit of spit on the cake. Everybody got a big piece—my favorite, of course, yellow with chocolate frosting—with chocolate ice cream scooped over the top.

Then Dad announced, "Okay—everyone in the living room for presents. That is, if anyone's gotten him any!"

This led to a huge chorus of "I didn't, did you?" "Oh, I thought you were getting him something." "Wow, this is really embarrassing!"

I pretended to be hurt, but I was actually more excited about the surprise we had planned for Chive than anything else. We gathered around the coffee table, which was piled high with packages, and everyone started giving me directions about what to open first.

I got a comb from Old Lou, and a pair of handmade woolen mittens from Grandma—just what I needed for the summer. Mom and Dad gave me some shorts and new hightops, which Chive and I high-fived over. I finally got to Al's before he had a coronary—a videotape of the last World Skateboard Championships. I knew we'd be spending a lot of time in front of the VCR going over this one.

I was telling everyone how much I liked all my stuff when P.B. tugged at my sleeve. "I brought you a present, too, Terry."

He dug into his pocket and pulled out a stick of Juicy Fruit gum that he must have been carrying around for weeks. It was losing its paper wrapping and felt stiff as a board—like one snap would crumble it into a hundred pieces. "Hey, how'd you know this was my favorite?"

"Well, I didn't for sure," he said, "but I figured it looked like a good one, so I saved it for you."

"Tell you what—you and I'll share it sometime next week during practice."

"I got you a little something too." Chive pressed a small package into my hand. It was wrapped neatly in newspaper and held together with a piece of string that ended in a bow on top.

I held it for a moment, and everyone got real quiet. "Are these my best double hightop laces back? Because I sure could use them for my new sneaks."

Chive laughed and turned red.

I started to open it, but my hands had gone all fumbly. Finally I turned back the last fold of newspaper and pulled out what was inside. It was a whistle carved out of wood—soft, honey-colored wood. The perfectly rounded tube had a tapered mouthpiece at one end and a band of raised stars at the other, and the whole thing had been polished so smooth it almost sparkled. And it was threaded onto one of my old red hightop laces!

"I thought maybe you could use it to set up each of our team's tricks," said Chive shyly.

"What a great idea!" said Al, hopping to his feet. *"Tweet!"* he blew an imaginary whistle. "Into the leapfrog! *Tweet-tweet*—follow the leader!"

"The workmanship on that thing is incredible," said Dad.

"I know who made it," P.B. offered. Chive gave him a kick.

We all looked at Chive to see if he was going to tell us where it had come from, but all he said was, "I've got a friend who does whittling for the fun of it. I asked him to make it for you."

"Well, this is the best," I said, looking him straight in the eye. I could tell he was having a hard time looking back, but he didn't blink. I threw the shoelace and whistle around my neck and gave Dad a little shove. It was time.

Dad got up and went to the hall closet while everybody took turns blowing my whistle and just about strangling me to death.

"Well, Chive," Dad said, standing next to him with a long, flat box in his arms. "You've been around this house quite a bit these days, you know."

Chive blushed and said, "Yes, sir. I know it. Hope I haven't worn out my welcome."

"No, not yet," Dad went on. "We'll let you know when you do." We all laughed. "Anyway, we don't know when your birthday is, so we decided to give you your present now so we'd be sure not to miss it." He placed the box on Chive's lap.

Chive stared at it, frozen. He started to lift it, like he was looking for someone to pass it to, but Mom pushed it back toward him. "Go on, open it. You're worse than Terry."

We began chanting, "Open it! Open it! Open it!"

He tore into the package with both hands, paper flying all over the place. Then with one huge tug he ripped open the top and looked into the box. "It's a skateboard," he whispered.

"Of course, it's a skateboard, you dummy!" I said. "You're going to be in a skateboard tournament, aren't you?"

"This is a beauty," said Al, and he pulled it from the box since it didn't look like Chive could move his arms.

"It's a skateboard," Chive whispered again. Then he jumped to his feet, grabbed the board away from Al, and yelled, "I'm going to try it out!"

Al and I were right behind him, picking up our boards on the way, and P.B. came running after us.

We were halfway out the door when we heard Dad shout "Hold your horses!"

We stopped but stayed in motion, shifting from one foot to the other.

"It's pretty cool out there. Shouldn't you be wearing jackets or something?"

"Nah, Dad."

"I'm not cold."

"I don't really think we need jackets, Mr. Caldwell."

"Not even these?" Mom asked.

We all turned around and lost our breath at the same time. There stood Mom and Dad holding three red satin jackets that read TRIPLE THREAT ON WHEELS in white stitching across the back. Then they flipped them over, so we could see that each jacket had one of our names sewn on the left shoulder. We dove toward them, throwing our arms into the sleeves and fumbling with the zippers. Suited up, we stared at each other. Chive especially kept looking down at his name, almost with a frown.

Then Dad topped it off by producing from behind his back a red satin hat in P.B.'s size that said MASCOT on the visor.

"Let's do it!" I yelled, and we went tearing out onto the lighted driveway for a super practice.

After what seemed like only a few minutes, Mom stuck her head out the door and said it was ten-thirty already and Mr. Drucker was on his way over to pick up Al. P.B. asked if he could sleep in the same room with Chive and me that night, so we put him in my bed and made up a combination of sleeping bags and blankets on the floor for ourselves.

"Let's tell ghost stories," P.B. said two seconds before he started snoring. But Chive and I lay awake in the dark, too wound up to sleep.

"I think we've got the leapfrog down solid, don't you?" I whispered.

"Oh, yeah," he said, "that one's a snap. We've

got to come up with one more good one before the tournament, though. Maybe something like a human pinwheel."

"You never quit, do you?"

"Nope. I can't."

I had a feeling he was talking about more than skateboarding now, and we were quiet for a few minutes. It seemed like the right moment for a big question, so I took my chances. "Chi-ive . . ." I said, turning his name into two syllables. "If you're living on the street . . ." I heard the sleeping bag rustle and hoped he wasn't getting ready to make a run for it. "I mean, if you are—I'm not asking you straight out or anything—but if you are, can't you find a place to stay in one of those homes or something? I mean, wouldn't that be better—at least for a while?"

Chive sighed deeply in the darkness. "It's not that easy, Ter."

I held my breath, waiting for more.

"Hey, thanks for the skateboard. And happy birthday, old man. You sleep good, now."

"Night," I whispered back.

It was definitely beginning to get to me. There was something about being with Chive that made me feel—helpless. Here I had all this stuff, and he hardly had anything. I mean, I could give him my hand-me-down clothes and a new skateboard for his "birthday" and feed him dinner and give him someplace to sleep for the night—sometimes.

But I knew when it came right down to it, I couldn't give him my home or my parents or my school—any of the things that a kid needs to grow up. He was on his own for all that. And I hated it a lot.

CHIVE

August 18, 1991

"Hey, Pop! Look what I got for you!" I blurted out as soon as I saw his hand push aside the wooden plank that was the only thing separating our latest hiding place from the street. I could see by Pop's face that I had given him a bit of a scare, so I waited for him to wriggle into the crawl space before adding, "It's a pork chop." He put the plank back into place. "It's pretty good too. I got it last night from a lady I met."

I didn't want to be asked right yet why I was talking all of a sudden, so I just kept going. "Oh, yeah, and we've got company. They're back in there— asleep, I think. They wanted to stay up to meet you, but I told them you'd still be here in the morning."

Pop frowned and started for the back of the crawl space, which led into the bigger room. "It's okay," I said. "They're only kids. Little ones." I held the foil-wrapped pork chop out to him. "Can we go outside to talk?" I asked.

He took the package from me and nodded, and I followed him out until we were sitting on the curb. For a while he sat there and nibbled at the chop without looking at me. I figured this was his way of taking all this news in before he said anything himself. But that was okay. I needed some time to go over in my head what I wanted to say too.

"This *is* good," he finally said. "Thanks for saving it for me. Where did you say you got it?"

"At this lady's house. I helped her load her groceries a couple of times, and yesterday she invited me home for dinner, so I went. I almost ended up staying the night too. She was nice."

"I see." He took another bite. "So, where'd you tell her your family was, Son?" Pop's voice sounded shaky.

"I told her I didn't know where you were. Well, I didn't exactly!"

Pop jumped at hearing my voice so loud, and I remembered the kids sleeping inside. "I didn't really lie," I went on in a strong whisper. "I didn't bother telling her the whole truth, that's all. I said I couldn't stay because you might come back looking for me."

Pop sighed and shook his head.

"Well, you did, didn't you?"

I saw a small smile start to break over Pop's face, but then he sobered up so fast, I knew I wasn't out of the woods yet. "It's not right, Son," he said. "We don't live off other people like that. We may be poor, but we're not beggars."

"It's not begging!" I heard myself yell. Pop tried to put his arm around me, but I pulled away. "It's not begging!" I screamed again. "She offered me a home-cooked meal, and all I did was not turn her down! And it wasn't even for me! It was for those kids back there. I didn't have enough food to feed them all weekend, and sure enough, the lady sent me back with leftovers. Besides, if she took me in, maybe she'll take in another kid sometime. Do you know there're bunches of them roaming around by them-selves out there? Little kids, I mean. Some of them have mommas, but some of them I'm not so sure about."

Pop kind of winced when I said that.

"This little girl—her name's Maria, and she's got an awful cold."

Pop cleared his throat, and I stopped talking. I knew we were both thinking about Sarry.

"Okay," he said. "They can stay here with us as long as they like. But we're going to have to come up with some way of putting more food on the table."

"Pop . . ." I started.

"And we'll have to be more careful around the Arms. If those welfare folks think I'm harboring other people's children, they'll come down on us hard—"

"Pop!" I said a little louder to get his attention. He stopped, surprised, and let me finish. "Pop, you can't be part of this. You'll only be in the way. Do you remember that time you went to the vegetable stand to try and get us some old fruit, and the grocer chased you away?"

Pop frowned, and I hurried on. "And then I went back the next day by myself, and he gave me all kinds of good stuff—fresh too?"

Pop nodded, and I shrugged. "It's easier for a kid, Pop. People feel sorry for kids. I know you want to help, but I think this is something I have to do by myself."

"Well, I can't have you going willy-nilly into strange people's houses. It's not safe!"

"It's safer than out here," I said. "I'm careful, Pop. I wouldn't go home with just anybody."

Pop looked down at his hands for a moment, then raised one to scrub across my brush cut. "How'd you get so grown-up all of a sudden?" he asked. "And now that you've found your voice, are you ever going to let me get a word in edgewise again?"

I giggled.

"Okay," he said. "If you've got a plan, let's hear it."

I scrunched around to face him. "All right. First thing we've got to do is find a hiding place that's more permanent. . . ."

TERRY

June 6, 1992

The day of the tournament was perfect. The sun was out good and strong, but the air was still cool. Not much wind, nice dry pavement. The stands were almost packed. Old Lou kept screaming out "Terry!" to make sure I knew where she and Mom and Dad were sitting. And I could see Mr. Drucker popping a new tape into his video camera.

The only person who wasn't there was P.B. Chive said his mother had showed up for him last night and was taking him someplace for the weekend. Great timing. Chive said he didn't even look all that thrilled about going with her. I missed him, although I had to admit it was a lot quieter without him around.

I looked up and down our bench to see if any of the other guys had jackets as cool as ours, but I couldn't tell. If they did, they were probably hiding them like we were until it was our turn to show. That was Chive's idea—he was firm about it too— said it would make for a bigger impact when we skated out into the arena.

So, we sat there on the benches designated for contestants, our gear bags with our jackets in them between our feet, rubbing our boards down with a cloth we passed back and forth between us. I knew Chive and Al were doing exactly what I was at that moment—going over moves in their heads, thinking out the areas where we had the most trouble. They had even more to worry about than I did. At the last minute I had decided to drop out of the solo competition. I had worked pretty hard on my routine, but in no way did it match up to either of theirs. Besides, as elected captain of the Triple Threat on Wheels, I had enough responsibility on my shoulders. I could hardly wait to get out there. We were going to knock their socks off.

At last the chairman of the Department of Parks stood up. "Ladies and gentlemen," he said into the booming microphone. "We have assembled here some of the best young skateboarders you'd ever want to see. I know they're the best because they're from our fine county."

Everybody cheered and started bouncing around on the benches. This crowd was psyched.

"Today you're going to see demonstrations in solo skateboarding, doubles skateboarding—and we even hear that there is a three-man team this year!"

There was some applause for that, and Al, Chive, and I elbowed each other so hard, we almost fell off the bench.

"The contestants are good; the stakes are high. So, gentlemen—and ladies"—he nodded to the few girls who sat with us—"let's skate!"

Everyone cheered again, and over the noise the chairman announced that they would begin with the multiple-board events.

We watched several two-man teams come out and do their stuff. They were all pretty much the same, doing the usual crisscrosses and side-by-sides. A couple of girls had put together a routine with a bunch of fancy dance steps thrown in, but we knew they didn't have the technical moves the judges were looking for. We kept looking at each other and shaking our heads—this was going to be a piece of cake. There was one team, though, that got our attention. They were fast on their boards and had on matching polo shirts and shorts. For their finale they did this great trick where they lined up one in front of the other. Then the front guy tipped the nose of his board up into a two-foot wheelie while the back guy tipped his board down and grabbed his partner's waist, creating the first known two-man, two-board wheelie. It got a big hand from the audience.

Then we heard the chairman saying, "And now,

one of this afternoon's biggest treats—they call themselves the Triple Threat on Wheels—here they come, ladies and gentlemen!" Another one of Chive's ideas—not using our names, just the team title. He said it gave us an air of mystery. I said it was dumb, but Al liked it, too, so I gave in.

We hauled our jackets from the bags, slapped each other's hands once for good luck, and skated out into the arena—Chive at one end, Al in the middle, and me at the other end. I took a couple of deep breaths and let out a strong toot on my whistle. Al and I bent over with our legs spread apart while Chive came charging at us from behind. Reaching Al, he jumped off his board, letting it sail between Al's legs while he leapfrogged over Al's back. Then he landed on his board and got ready for his second jump over me. I felt his hands spring off my back and saw him bend over at an angle in front of me. Now it was Al's turn, and he jumped over me and Chive and took his place at the front of the line. By the time I was doing my own leapfrog over Chive, the crowd was really into it. We completed a full circle around the arena with the sound of clapping and shouting in our ears.

I gave my whistle a short blast and backed my board into a corner of the field. Al and Chive divided the rest of the arena into even thirds and turned to face me. Another toot on the whistle and Al and I started toward each other. I hit two short blasts, and we both flew up in the air at the same time and landed on each other's boards. I skated toward Al's old place, spun around, and stopped. Al made a small circle and turned to meet Chive, who was coming at him. Two more blasts and another successful exchange was made. Then it was Chive's and my turn. I hit the whistle and leapt into the air, but spotting down on Chive's board, I misjudged the distance by a fraction. As I landed, I felt the board start to skid out from under my left foot. A few people gasped. Don't lose it now, kid. With a slight dip I pulled up with my right hip, and the board straightened out again. The crowd cheered, and I raised my fist in triumph.

Then we went into our easier stuff to give ourselves a break—follow-the-leader kick turns, twisting around each other in braids, and what we called our "radar scope" chorus line with Chive running the widest part of the circle, me in the middle, and Al doing 360s in the center.

Our five minutes were almost up, so I blew three short blasts, and Chive and I moved toward center field to meet Al. We nodded to each other, and Al mumbled, "Try not to hit my butt."

That almost gave us an attack of the giggles, but we managed to get serious again, and I blew the whistle. At the same time we all turned our right shoulders toward each other and started skating in a tight circle. When we were up to speed and perfectly aligned, I gave another short toot, and we grabbed each other's wrists—my hand over

Chive's, his over Al's, and Al's over mine. One more blast and we rocked our boards back onto the rear wheels, and there it was, ladies and gentlemen—the human pinwheelie! The product of weeks of practice that had included scraped ankles, wrenched arms, and as Al put it, bruised butts from boards that flew out of control.

A short whistle and we disconnected and flattened out our boards. With everyone still clapping and screaming we fanned out into a straight line, and as I blew one last time, we all kicked down onto our boards, sending them as high into the air as they would go. I moved quickly from the right to the center; Al moved to the left; and Chive, being the fastest, ran around to my right. Then, as if there were nothing to it, we watched the boards float down into our waiting hands.

The crowd jumped to its feet, and we stood in the center of the arena, arms up, boards above our heads. I grinned over to where Al's parents and mine and Old Lou were jumping up and down and carrying on and then scanned the seats for other friends and their families. That's when I saw him— this guy standing a little ways off from everybody else in the bleachers. He had on these goofy overalls and a T-shirt, and he was smiling and clapping his hands over his head. He looked familiar, but I couldn't remember where I knew him from.

The applause finally started to die down, and we made our way, arm-punching and high-fiving, back to the benches. We took off our sweaty jackets, passed a towel around for our faces, and waited for the judges to make their decision.

"Okay, we have a doubles winner!" the chairman said, waving a piece of paper.

"Get on with it," Al said between his teeth.

"Glen Pfeiffer and Mark Denham!" It was the polo shirts!

"No way!" I said.

Al threw the towel down between his feet. "Oh, man—what a rip!"

Chive pressed his lips together and frowned.

The chairman leaned over the mike again. "Now we move on to the single-board event!"

"Come on, you guys," I said. "You've got to keep it together for the solos." Already I was trying to forget that I'd just lost my only shot at a prize.

"In this competition solo skateboarders will be awarded points for the number of moves completed, as well as the degree of difficulty, originality, and execution of the overall routine."

We watched four men move a large wooden ramp to the end of the arena. The bottom section would be used for ollies and low jumps, while the higher end leveled into a platform for more complicated takeoffs.

"When are we going to get a real half-pipe?" grumbled Al.

"What's that?" asked Chive.

"It's this humongous curved ramp the heavy-duty skaters ride," I explained.

Actually, this thing looked scary enough, and I was glad I had decided to leave this part of the tournament to Al and Chive, who were nervously licking their lips, shaking out their shoulders, and retying their sneakers. Chive was also checking the tape on the gauze padding that Mom had wrapped around his ankle. She had been doctoring that cut of his with salve, and it was almost healed. Naturally she wanted it to stay that way.

"Number one, ladies and gentlemen, is David Karp. Let's give him a welcoming hand." The big race was underway, and there was some stiff competition here. This kid Karp got off to a good start with a lot of clean skating, great turns, and a kick flip ending off the platform that made Al groan, "Time to go home." Even Chive looked a little pale. Luckily not everyone was that good. But you could tell they had all done their homework.

"Number eighteen, Allen Drucker!"

I gave Al a push, and Chive called after him, "Kick butt!" And he did. All those months on his driveway and mine paid off. He began with a series of 180s, stringing them together nice and smooth—like it was all one motion. Then he did an L-sit into a coffin, making everyone laugh as he glided across the concrete on his back, hands folded solemnly over his heart. After that he got the board rolling fast enough for him to do a low lean off to the side. Around the circle he went, hanging so far over the edge I thought he was going to dump himself onto his shoulder. But he held it, and I heard his dad yell, "Atta boy!"

A squat-nose wheelie, a few of his best backward kick turns, and he wheeled up the ramp for his final jump, an air walk. He crouched down, ready to grab the board with one hand while his left leg straightened out in front and his right leg stretched back. As he lifted off, his red jacket flared out like wings, and for a moment he looked like a cardinal buzzing the arena. Then board and feet came down for a perfect landing, and his face lit up as the crowd roared its approval. Boy, it looked like he had this thing nailed! But Chive was up next.

"Now we come to number nineteen—Jay Flory!" Jay Flory? Al and I looked at the number taped to Chive's shirt—it was nineteen, all right.

Chive shrugged and said, "Well, I'm going out there."

While I was still trying to figure it out, Chive was already on a roll. Al whistled encouragement as Chive wasted no time in getting his board up to speed. He started out with a bunch of kick turns then lifted the nose of the board until he was spacewalking. A couple more strong push-offs, and he was walking the board, his feet crisscrossing back and forth as he worked his way down the middle of the field.

"He probably gets it from dodging bums in that dump where he lives," Al said in my ear.

"Ease off, dork—I don't see you dancing like that."

Chive did some ollies up the bottom edge of the ramp—just like the ones Al had shown him—and then rolled out into a G-turn. He was moving! He followed with a combination of wheelies, some reverse 180s, and I don't know how many 360s. I was counting, and so far he had done more moves than any other skater that afternoon.

I glanced over to see how the judges were reacting to Chive's performance, and my eyes stopped. There was that overalls guy again. He was leaning forward on his seat, punching one hand into the other and moving his lips like he was saying, "Go! Go!" I got a good look at his face this time. It was leathery, and his eyes were kind of sunk into his head. And he had this uneven brush cut with streaks of gray going through the sandy color. He looked like—ohmigosh—he looked like Chive! The crowd's shouts pulled my attention back to the arena.

Chive was revving up for his final jump off the platform. But he fooled us by sliding right by it. He circled around the back and came to a full stop off to the side, where the ramp angled above the ground at a height of about three feet. Then he backed up a few inches, his eyes riveted to the open space below the ramp. What was he going to do, slide under it? No, he was going to jump over it sideways! He took off and started building up speed, coming so close to the edge, I thought he was going to get it right in the stomach. But just before impact he lifted into the air, his legs pulled up under him, leaving the board to glide without him under the slope of the ramp. Over the top he went, the board disappearing from his sight for a crucial two seconds. Then down he came—kid and board together once again—and Al and I joined the crowd as it rose to its feet. What a move!

Chive sailed to the center of the arena for what we expected to be his finish—but, no, he was bending over. Had he lost his balance so close to the end? Al and I clutched each other's arms like it was us falling. Then our mouths fell open and we stared. Chive was riding the board on his hands. Correction—one hand. That's when we knew we were seeing something totally amazing. Here was a kid who had never even seen a board until a couple months ago, and now he was cleaning up this tournament like a pro. He pulled himself up to a sharp stop and grabbed the board to his chest. People were going nuts! I looked up behind me to where my parents were sitting. Dad gave me a wink while Mom did her famous whistle through her fingers. Old Lou was screaming, "Chive! Chive!"

"I don't believe he did it!" I yelled to Al over my own clapping.

"I do," he said, shaking his head and smiling. "I taught that kid everything I know. Way to go, veggie!"

But Chive couldn't hear him because a bunch of people had rushed down to lift him onto their shoulders and deliver him to the judging stand. I gave him the thumbs-up sign as he was carried past, but he didn't see me. He was kind of frowning and didn't look too happy about all the attention he was getting.

"Well, we've got ourselves a winner by unanimous decision!" the chairman boomed. "Number nineteen—Jay Flory!"

"Chive!" I tried to correct the chairman, but I might as well have whispered it with all that noise.

He seemed to be studying his feet as the chairman brought him forward to give him his prize. Great time to go shy on us, Chivo!

"Well, congratulations, Jay," the chairman said. "And I guess you're pretty happy about winning these two hundred-dollar bills, young man." He held the bills up for everyone to see.

"Yes, sir, I am," Chive raised his head long enough to say. The chairman handed him the money, and he stuffed it into his jeans pocket. I was surprised he wasn't still wearing his jacket and realized for the first time that he hadn't worn it throughout his whole routine. I looked down and saw it hanging over the bench beside me.

"And here's your trophy," the chairman went on, "proclaiming you the best skateboarder in Perkins County. You certainly earned it."

Chive ducked his head in thanks again.

"We have one more prize to give out today," the chairman said, stepping in front of Chive. "I would like the members of the Triple Threat on Wheels to come forward at this time."

I grabbed Al, who looked kind of stunned, and started pushing my way to the judges' stand. For a second I thought of running back to get Chive's jacket, but it was too late. We climbed up onto the podium and took our places on either side of the chairman.

"These three young men have given us an excellent demonstration in discipline and team spirit. The judges have decided to award each of them fifty dollars for their mastery of this difficult sport."

I let out a whoop, and Al raised his arms, Rocky-style, over his head. We all thanked the chairman and took our money. Then several people closed in for some pictures, and we straightened our jackets and put on our biggest smiles.

"Come on, champ," I said, reaching behind me for Chive. My hand waved around but hit nothing. I wheeled full circle. He wasn't there. "Wait a second." I held my hands up to stop the photographers. "We're missing one. Al, you see him?"

Al shrugged.

I looked down behind the stand and then out into the arena again. There was no way I was going to spot him in the crowd that was now swarming all over the pavement.

I felt a tug on one of my socks and saw Old Lou leaning out of Mom's arms to reach me. "Chive!" she shouted.

"I'm Terry," I said. "Mom, have you seen Chive? Some people want to take our picture."

"Well, he was right here a second ago. Wasn't he wonderful? Well, you all were!"

I looked straight across the field to where the man with the brush cut had been sitting. He was gone too. So what? I was missing one kid and one weird guy. It didn't have to add up to anything. A few more pictures and handshakes and we were almost ready to come down to reality.

I went over to get Chive's jacket but couldn't find it. I looked around again, trying to pick out the shiny red on Chive's back. Nope. Well, I hoped he'd gotten it okay.

Al got a ride with us since his parents had to leave right after the prizes were given out in order to get home and walk their ancient dog. But neither of us seemed to have much to say once we were in the car. Mom and Dad kept going on and on about our performance, and Old Lou crawled all over us until I asked Mom to make her stop.

When we got to Al's house, I said, "I'll skate home if that's okay with you guys." They let us out, and Al and I started walking to his front door.

"So, what're you going to do with your fifty dollars?" Al asked, kicking a piece of gravel up the driveway with his toe.

"I don't know—maybe buy some Rollerblades."

"You serious?"

I shrugged.

"Why'd he take off like that, anyway?"

"Beats me. Maybe he had someplace to go."

"After winning first prize in a skateboard tournament? Like where?"

"I don't *know*. Stop bugging me!" I slid my foot over and took the piece of gravel away from him.

"Well, I don't get it. We show him all our moves, you give him a board that does everything but skate by itself—I mean, we spent almost every day together! Then he wins a big wad of dough, and bingo, he's gone. You'd think he'd at least have treated us to dinner at McDonald's. I'm starving. You want to come in for something to eat?"

"Nah, I'm going on home." I gave the piece of gravel one last kick, and it landed in Mrs. Drucker's flower bed. "Sorry about that," I said.

"Well, see you tomorrow."

"I guess."

Al went into the house, and I stood there for a couple of minutes. This was dumb. This was supposed to be one of the greatest days of our lives, and now Chive had to go and spoil it.

I turned and walked back down the driveway, making a right at the end and kicking my board ahead of me in the direction of home. As I walked, I took off my jacket and stuffed it in my gear bag. I was sick of wearing it already.

CHIVE

June 6, 1992

It felt strange to be inside the supermarket instead of out in the parking lot, like I usually was. I was glad the store was almost empty except for me and a few folks who looked like they were just getting off the night shift. I had never been grocery shopping by myself before, and I didn't want anybody staring at me or anything.

I turned down the first aisle, pushing the empty cart. Cookies! This part was easy—two bags of Oreos—make that three—and a couple of packages of chocolate chip for good measure. They wouldn't last long, but I couldn't spend all my prize money on cookies. And there was the peanut butter. Four large jars of chunky ought to do it, if I could get P.B. to share it with the others. Some cans of tuna, more baked beans. Canned carrots, peas, beets, corn. Nobody'd thank me for these, but the kids had to have *some* healthy stuff.

Four big bottles of soda pop, some potato chips, a few apples, three loaves of bread, cheese, and a couple gallons of milk. No point in getting too much—the milk would only spoil. I counted the things in my cart. That should hold us for a while. Besides, I didn't want to buy more than I could carry. I also didn't want to attract attention by flashing around a lot of cash.

I thought back to earlier that evening, when Pop and I had gone into the Brew & Burger to have something to drink and break one of the hundred-dollar bills. I sipped on a tall, cold Coke while Pop had himself a Budweiser and counted the change. Then he handed over the whole amount to me, saying, "And don't forget to save fifty cents of that for your college education." I hadn't heard him say that in a long time.

Now I pulled up into the only check-out line that was open and started piling my stuff onto the conveyor belt. The cashier looked like she could be somebody's grandma. "Ma'am," I asked as politely as possible, "do you suppose it would be all right if I borrowed this cart long enough to take these bags home? I'm not sure I'm going to be able to carry them all by myself, and my momma is laid up in bed with the flu."

She looked at me kind of sideways as she tallied up my groceries. "I'm surprised your mother let you out of the house this time of night. You got money to pay for all this?"

"Yes, ma'am. How much?" I decided I'd better not say anything else about my momma with Grandma here keeping such a close eye on me. "Really, ma'am. I've got the money." I fanned a few bills out in front of her.

"Sixty-three seventy-two," she said without smiling.

I whistled a long, low note. Two hundred and fifty wasn't going to last long at this rate. I pulled out four twenties and handed them to her. "How about the cart, ma'am? I can bring it back around in half an hour tops."

"It'll wait until morning. No point in your being out any later than you already are. It's not my cart anyway—take it."

I smiled at her and pushed the cart toward the supermarket door before she changed her mind. Once outside, I patted my jeans pocket to make sure I still had Pop's knife on me. It *was* late, even for me. Then I got a good running start and pulled my feet up on the rungs above the wheels so I could ride the cart down the street a bit.

When I reached our building, I left the cart on the sidewalk long enough to lean through the doorway and holler up the stairs. "Hey!" I knew this was risky, but it was either that or take the chance that someone would make off with one of the grocery bags while I was carrying the other two up the stairs. P.B. hung his head over the second-story railing. "Hey," I called again, this time a little softer. "I thought you were with Linda."

"She brought me back early. I saw your trophy—do you get to keep it? I made a new friend."

"P.B," I said, "I've got four big jars of peanut butter down here. Are you going to come and get them, or should I leave them for the rats?"

P.B. came bounding down the stairs, followed by Missy and a kid I'd never seen before.

"This is Pete," P.B. said, jerking his thumb at the boy behind him.

He sure didn't look like one of our usual visitors. He was wearing a leather vest with metal studs running down the front, and his black jeans looked new. He was also a good head taller than I was.

I smiled and stuck out my hand. "Hi, Pete. My name's Chive."

He smiled back but left my hand hanging in the air. "Oh? I thought it was Jay. I saw you today at the skateboard tournament," he said. "You're pretty good. Got yourself a nice piece of change for it, too, didn't you?"

That was all I needed to hear. "Everybody upstairs!" I shouted. P.B. and Missy froze with their hands still in the shopping bags. "Go!" I yelled again, and they scooted past me. Pete's smile turned into a smirk. "I think you must be looking for somebody else," I said, hoping he couldn't hear the shakiness in my voice.

"I don't. You've got some sweet setup here," he said, leaning against the doorframe and blocking my exit from the building. "You dealin'? Crack? Maybe a little smoke?"

"Nope," I said and hooked my thumbs in my jeans pockets.

"Yeah, well—I am." He laughed. "And I could use a front like you. Cute little bunch of kids, food delivered right to the door." He nodded at the groceries in the cart behind him and reached over to pull a bottle of soda out of one of the bags.

"Drop that," I said.

Pete laughed again. "Why should I? I get thirsty, too, you know. Oh, and by the way, I'll take the rest of that prize money you got on you. No sense in you spendin' it all on this kind of junk." He lunged at me and grabbed my shirt front.

My hands flew from my pockets, but I made sure the right one had the knife in it. As I had practiced a hundred times, I snapped my wrist and prayed I'd hear the blade clicking into place. At the same time I brought my hand up until the flat of the knife rested on Pete's arm.

"Hey, man!" Pete jumped back, letting go of my shirt. "Does your mommy know you're wavin' that thing around people?" He laughed nervously.

"I know how to use it," I whispered as I folded into a crouch and pointed the knife straight at his stomach.

"Yeah, sure you do," he said, but he didn't come

any closer. "Look, you're gonna be sorry for treatin' me this way, man. I'm comin' back with some friends of mine, and next time you're gonna need more than your little Boy Scout knife there." He turned to go, and as he passed the grocery cart, he pushed it over, sending food all over the street.

I waited until I was sure he was gone before I straightened up and bent the knife blade back into its handle. I sure hoped Pete was bluffing about coming back. I didn't like the fact that he had recognized me and followed me to our hideout. He must have seen me and Pop come out of the Brew & Burger. That's what I got for not being more careful. I'd let myself get too carried away with the tournament—not taking care of business, as Pop would say. Well, all that was over now.

It would be a real hassle if I had to move everybody again because of this Pete guy. It was hard to find a good place, and besides, I worried that the mothers and kids wouldn't know where to look for me. I'd have to gamble on my hunch that we were too small-time for Pete to bother with.

I bent down to see how much damage had been done to our food and was glad to find that most of it looked all right. Of course, now I was definitely going to have to carry it up all by myself, one armload at a time. I picked through the bags, leaving one jar of peanut butter that had shattered and a bag of chips that was soaking up a dirty puddle in the street.

Five trips up and down the stairs later, I sat in our room, serving up a midnight supper.

"Show us the trick with the ramp again," Missy begged through a mouthful of tuna fish and bread.

"No, that's enough for tonight." I looked over at the red satin jacket hanging from a rusty nail in the faded flowered wallpaper. The bottom tip of a sleeve dusted the top of the trophy that sat below it. It seemed like years since I had been skating in that arena in front of all those people.

"Your pop says you were terrific," said a little bit of a guy we named Socks, mostly because he kept losing his. "Too bad he had to miss all this neat food."

I nodded. "Yep, it sure is—but he had to get back to work. I don't know how he talked the supervisor into giving him time off to come to the tournament anyway. He shouldn't mess around with jobs like that—weekends pay good overtime, and we need all the cash we can get."

"Oh, I almost forgot!" yelled Hatter, spitting potato chips. "Mrs. Marsh said to give you this." I frowned at Hatter, who blinked at me from underneath the baseball cap he even slept in. He dug around in his pocket until he came up with two wadded bills, which he passed to me.

I unfolded them and whistled. "Forty dollars! She shouldn't be doing that."

"I didn't ask for it!" Hatter said, his eyes wide.

"I know you didn't." I winked at him. "She's a nice lady, isn't she?"

"Yeah, I like her. She let me play in the attic, and Henry took me for a ride in the big car. She asked me when you and I are going to move in with her, and I didn't know what to say. I know I'm not supposed to tell her about my mom and dad."

I winced. It was one thing for me to stretch the truth, but I hated making the little ones lie too. "You did good—I'll take care of it, okay?"

"I'm sorry about Pete," P.B. mumbled into the peanut butter jar he was hugging.

"That's all right," I said. "But next time, let me talk to anyone you don't know before you invite them upstairs."

"So, how much money you got left, Chive?" asked Froggie without looking up from the cheese sandwich he was building.

"Well—including the forty we just got from Mrs. Marsh—probably about two hundred and twenty bucks."

"That settles it," said Froggie. "I'm eating here from now on."

"Me too," said Socks. "I hate that stuff you get in the food lines. Last week they said it was beef stew, and it didn't even look like real meat."

"Somebody told me they use horsemeat," added P.B.

"They do not," said Socks.

"Do too."

"Do not."

"Do too."

I leaned back and banged my head against the wall a few times while the kids stopped chewing and watched. When I tilted forward again, I had to laugh at the worry on their faces and said as gently as I could, "I'm glad we're having this party tonight. But I want you guys to remember that this food is for emergencies only. My prize money won't last forever, and we shouldn't be counting on handouts from Mrs. Marsh. The main thing is still for you to eat and sleep in some nice home any night you can, get it? And right now this party is over so we all can get up early tomorrow and meet some new people. I've been spending so much time getting ready for the tournament that I don't think I was at the market parking lot more than twice last week. That's no good. So, okay—everybody gets one Oreo and a swig of milk, and it's bedtime."

Missy peered inside the cookie bag when it was her turn. "Could we save one of these for my mom? I think they're her favorites."

"Why don't you keep one for her?" She hesitated. "Go on," I said, pushing the bag toward her. "I believe you."

Missy shook her head. "I'm afraid I'll roll over on it in my sleep and smush it."

"Okay. You hear that, you guys!" I held up the bag. "We're saving one of these cookies for Missy's mom."

"Yeah, and one for my uncle Joe!"

"How about my dog, Chive—he loves Oreos!"

They all started hooting and hollering until I had to raise my voice louder than theirs to be heard.

"That's it!" The ruckus lowered to a buzzing, and the packing cardboards were laid out and jackets and sweatshirts arranged until everybody was bedded down.

When I was sure that they were mostly quiet, I stretched out and listened to the street noise outside. I wondered if Terry and Al were having their own party tonight. I also wondered if I'd ever see them again. I'd been away from the hideout too much lately. The kids needed me, and my other families were asking where I'd been. Besides, the more I stayed at Terry's, the harder it got to leave.

I got up and tiptoed over to my jacket. Lifting it carefully off the nail, I lay back down and draped it over my chest. The soft coolness against my arms put me right to sleep, and I dreamt I was back at the old skating rink, showing Sarry and Louanne how to skateboard on ice.

TERRY

June 17, 1992

"Hey, you guys, it's one of the Triple Threat on Wheels! Ya know, he don't look like much of a threat to me!"

I'd know Gary Samuels's voice out of all my worst nightmares, so I didn't even bother to turn around when I heard him behind me in the hall. I was late coming back from lunch and still had to get to my locker to pick up my social studies book.

"Hey, you—Caldwell! I hear you're givin' away skateboards. I could sure use one. Maybe even join the team—sounds like you could use a replacement!"

"Can I do something for you, Samuels?" I had reached my locker and wanted to put an end to this before he and his pack of creeps decided to clean it for me.

"Yeah, you can," Samuels said and winked at

Fat Frank, who stood like a concrete lump at his left side, and Markie Porter, the skinny weasel on his right. "You can tell me where I can get a deal like your poor little friend. Boy, moochin' off rich people all over town. Sounds good to me!" He laughed at his own joke, and Frank and Markie laughed, too, even though they probably didn't know what he was talking about.

The problem was I didn't know what he was talking about either. But he and his slimeballs were already shuffling down the hall, and I didn't want to call them back. I opened my locker and started to poke through the mess in search of my book. But I stopped when a piece of paper taped to the inside of the door caught my eye. There, alongside the picture of Guns and Roses and a Wheels Up decal that should have been on my board, was a note. It had to be from Al, because he was the only one who knew my combination. It said, "Meet me after school. News flash."

At four-thirty I found Al at our usual meeting place by the outside drinking fountain. "Hi," I said. "What's up?"

"Mr. Cabot gave us a pop quiz on this stupid poem we were supposed to memorize, and I think I blew it. My dad's going to have kittens if I bring home a C on my last report card."

"Is this the big news flash? Stop being so paranoid—you probably did fine. Hey, did you say anything to anybody about me giving Chive a skateboard? Gary Samuels and his goonies got to me in the hall today. He started going on about Chive mooching off rich people—I mean, I wouldn't exactly call my family rich . . ."

"But that's what I wanted to talk to you about."

"What?"

Al took a deep breath. "I don't think you're the only person who's had Chive over to their house for dinner and stuff."

"What do you mean?"

"I think he's been to Cathy Frascotti's too. A lot."

"That girl with the blond ponytail in Mrs. Monroe's class? Where'd he meet *her*?"

"She told Bobby Tabor that her mom brought home this weird kid from the supermarket over on Briar Ridge Road because he looked hungry—sound familiar? Anyway, Bobby heard me talking about how we met Chive and saw him all the time before the tournament. So, he put two and two together and—"

"Who were you talking to?"

"Gary Samuels?" said Al in a small voice.

"Great."

"I couldn't help it. He was asking a lot of questions, like who was the third guy on our skating team and was that the guy who won first prize and where did he come from . . ."

"What does this have to do with Chive having dinner at Cathy Frascotti's?"

"Well, now that the story's going around school,

some other kids say they've heard about the same kind of thing. You know, people feeding some kid they know nothing about, having him stay overnight. Someone even said it was a *girl*, and I told them 'No way.' "

I couldn't stand listening to this dumb gossipy stuff any longer. "Hey, look, maybe it was Chive," I said. "I'm not his mother—I don't keep his schedule for him. If he's hanging out someplace else now, that's his business."

"But Terry, it's not now."

"What do you mean, it's not now?"

"I mean—I mean, he's not hanging out someplace else *now*. He was hanging out someplace else *then*. At the same time he was with us—at your house. Don't you think it's kind of funny he never said anything about it? Cathy told Bobby it's definitely the same kid—she saw him at the tournament. He was over at her house all April, May. . . ."

"What's your point?"

Al looked down at his feet. "Some people think he used us—you know, so he could learn how to skate and win the prize money."

I sat down on the curb. "Let me get this straight. You're saying he's been staying with a whole bunch of other folks all along, and that we were just another free meal?"

Al snickered. "You said 'folks'—like Chive."

"I did not! And I don't believe it! If he was that

hungry, we would have fed him every night—he knew that! Besides, how many people do you think are going to drag home some raggedy kid who hangs out in a parking lot, huh?"

"Well, *you* did," Al said and sat down next to me.

He was right—we did. But that was different. At least I thought it was different. "Listen, you want to clear this whole thing up? We'll go talk to him."

"How? You know where he hides out?"

"No. We'll just have to start where everybody else seems to be finding him—at the supermarket. Tomorrow after school. You with me?"

Al got up and pushed the button on the water fountain to get a drink. "Yeah, I'm with you." He stood to one side, his thumb still pressing down on the button. "You know, you're not the only one who misses him, Ter."

I got up and took the drink he offered. "Meet me right here."

I took the long way home to give myself some time to think. If Chive didn't want to hang out with us anymore, that was his problem. But he was making me look like a jerk, and I didn't like it. By the time I reached our house, I was in a rotten mood. I slammed the kitchen door so hard, the glasses rattled in the cupboard.

"Chive!" I heard Old Lou squeal from somewhere in the living room. She came toddling out at a run.

"No!" I growled at her. "It's not Chive! It's me—Terry! Your brother! No Chive!"

"Terry!" Dad yelled, but it was too late. Old Lou sat down in the middle of the floor and started crying like somebody had mugged her teddy bear.

"I'm sorry," I grumbled. I made a pass at washing my hands and sat down at the table. "What's for dinner?"

"Not this," Dad said. "We're not having any more of this. Now, we're as disappointed as you are that Chive hasn't come around since the tournament. We probably never should have gotten involved with the boy in the first place. . . ." He shot a look at Mom. This wasn't going anywhere. I pushed my chair back from the table.

"I'm not hungry. I'll see you in the morning."

"Terry!" But Mom was calling to my back. I gave my bedroom door a good slam, too, and ended up having to put a pillow over my head to block out Old Lou's wailing.

CHIVE

June 17, 1992

"Meet me at McDonald's—6:00—Pop," read the note stuck in the heating vent behind the door. The heater in our hideout didn't work anymore, but it was a good place to leave messages where some nosy cop wouldn't see them.

Six o'clock! It was already twenty to six, and I was supposed to be at Mrs. Marsh's tonight. I had told her this big lie about losing my room at the Arms. Now I'd have to make up an even bigger one to explain why I hadn't shown up. Some days it was hard to keep my own stories straight. In the meantime I had two kids who had to be sent off to families, and food to be set out for the ones who were coming back.

"Tina, are you ready to go? Socks, you're going to have to walk her halfway to the Warnicks' on your way to the Praegers'. I've got to meet Pop somewhere." I started digging through our carton of canned goods.

"I thought he said he wouldn't be back until Friday," Socks said.

"You're right, he did. I hope they didn't lay him off the job again—we're running low on supplies here. Is this the last can of beans? Do you remember who's coming back tonight besides P.B., Bucky, and Missy?"

"Maybe Hatter."

"Well, they're going to have to make do with beans and peanut butter. And here's a can of beets."

Socks made a face. "I don't know why you keep buying those nasty old beets. You're the only one who likes them."

"I'll remember that. I guess this bread isn't too stale yet." I fished around in the bottom of the box until I found our only pen and ripped a piece off the shopping bag we used for notes. "Do not open the last bag of cookies!" I wrote and propped it up between the can of beans and the peanut butter jar.

"I've got to run," I said. "You both have a nice time tonight and be careful. Walk around the block instead of going past the Arms, okay? And wash Tina's hands and face at the hydrant before you go."

I did have to run for it now. I didn't know why Pop had picked McDonald's as a meeting place. It was almost halfway across town, and we couldn't afford to eat there. Maybe he'd heard of a new food line nearby that gave out big portions or something. I should have brought my board—I'd get there faster. But then, if Pop and I were going to a food line, it wouldn't look good to be carrying a shiny new skateboard under my arm. I did a leap off an invisible board and jumped over what would have been Terry's back. "Raaaahhh!" I whispered and raised my arms for the imaginary crowd. I dropped my arms again and concentrated on my running. I had to stop thinking about Terry and the tournament. It didn't do me any good.

When I got to McDonald's, Pop was nowhere in sight. I was looking up the side street for him when I heard a tapping noise behind me. There he was, sitting at a table inside the restaurant and waving at me like he was king of the world. He pointed to the door, and I went in.

"What are you doing here?" I asked as he motioned for me to sit down across from him.

"I got you a Quarter Pounder and some fries. They've got nice little apple pies, too, if you want some dessert. I couldn't remember whether you liked strawberry or chocolate shakes, so I got one of each. Which one do you want?"

This was the most I'd heard Pop talk since we left the farm. "Chocolate. Pop, what's going on?"

He slowly unwrapped one of the burgers and pushed it over to my side of the table. He then held up a little packet of ketchup and, when I nodded, squeezed the contents onto the fries. When he had everything the way he wanted it, he picked up his burger and before taking a bite said, "I got a job."

I looked at him suspiciously. "How many days?" I asked.

"Weeks, you mean," he said, licking mustard from the corner of his mouth. "Or *months*! How many months!" He laughed at my frowning face. "Okay, I've pulled your leg long enough. Eat your supper—it's getting cold."

I bit into my burger and waited.

"It's a real job," Pop said. His voice was soft, and he sounded like he was as surprised as I was by what he was saying. "The fellow running the last few construction jobs I've been on likes my work. Of course, it didn't hurt any that I happened to see the floor plans for this house we were building and noticed there was a mistake in the blueprints. I brought it to his attention, and he says I saved them thousands of dollars. So, Mr. O'Connell—that's the fellow's name—he asked me if I would be interested in a full-time job doing construction in Chicago, and I said I'd have to talk it over with you but that I would definitely give it some serious thought. It seems he's got a brother in that area who's looking to put together a construction crew to work on a series of housing developments in the suburbs. O'Connell thinks it might lead to something permanent, and I might even be able to supervise some of the projects. So, how about that?

You never know, do you?" He popped a fry into his mouth.

It was a dumb question, but I had to ask it anyway. "We're going to move?"

"Looks like it. And fast too. They'd like me to be there in three weeks if we can swing it. I told him I didn't see why not—nothing's holding us here."

I took another big bite of my burger so I wouldn't have to talk for a minute or two.

"Well, Son, I know it's a shock, but I thought you'd be a little more excited than this."

I knew I should be happy, but it was too much to think about all at once. "Where will we live?"

"Probably in an apartment at first. Then—who knows?—if things go well, maybe we'll be able to buy ourselves some kind of house. Have a backyard. I'll be one of those suburban farmers who plant little patches of tomatoes and zucchini."

"What about the kids?"

"Oh, I don't think you'll have any trouble meeting people, Chive. You'll be in school again, and I bet you'll find a lot of folks who'll be mighty impressed by what you can do on a skateboard."

"No! What about *our* kids? We can't just leave them like that!"

Pop ran a paper napkin across his mouth. "Well, I'm afraid we're going to have to, Chive. To begin with, they're *not* our kids. Of course, we'll tell all the mothers we can locate, and maybe some of—"

My fist came down on the table, and several

french fries bounced out of their box. "You don't even care! You've got a job now, and you're going to turn your back on them! You're just like everybody else, you know that?"

Pop grabbed for my wrist and held on to it so tightly, I felt the blood rush to my hand. "Lower your voice," he said. I looked around, and sure enough, people were staring at us. "You seem to have forgotten how to behave in a restaurant, Son." He let go of my wrist, and I rubbed it with my other hand.

"I do care about those kids. I'll miss them and worry about them as much as you—maybe more. But you couldn't have gone on much longer the way you were, having kids coming and going like that. And those families you were staying with— it was only a matter of time be—"

"Why not!" I shouted, forgetting how Pop's hand had felt on my wrist. "It's working, isn't it?"

"For the moment," Pop said, his voice low and even. "But did you think you could feed and house all the homeless children in this city? What if one of them got really sick or hurt at the hideout? How would you feel if a mother came back looking for her son or daughter, and you had to tell her something terrible had happened because you couldn't get the child to a hospital in time? How about their schooling? Were you going to be responsible for that too? See that they got to the dentist for checkups and had new shoes? And when this batch was all taken care of, would you be ready for the next group that came along? Because it's not going to end with these kids, you know. But you're the big hero—you've got it all figured out."

My face burned and I sputtered, "Well—well, at least I never turned any away!"

Pop opened his mouth, then closed it again and started folding his napkin into smaller and smaller squares. "Noooo, you never did that."

I brushed my hand across my eyes to get rid of the pictures that ran through my head—P.B. the first time I saw him rummaging in that garbage can; Socks showing up at the hideout with someone's handprint bruised across his back; and Sarry—always Sarry.

"Chive, this isn't about just you and me and our little band at the hideout. There's a whole network of systems that are supposed to take care of people like us. It all starts higher up—in some politician's fancy office. People vote and elect men and women they think will see to it that there are jobs and housing and health care enough for everybody in the country. But sometimes the politicians don't give us what they promise. The money gets into the wrong hands, and the systems break down. And it's up to the folks in this town to let the right people know that they're not going to stand by and watch while children fall through the cracks and end up living on the streets. Unfortunately one good-intentioned boy can't change all that by himself.

But I couldn't be prouder of you for trying. Now, come on—let's get some food for the kids. How many you got there tonight?"

"Four, I think," I said, following him to the take-out counter. "I'm supposed to be at Mrs. Marsh's."

"Well, if you said you'd be there, you probably should go. It's only seven—you can still make it. You should also start thinking about how you're going to tell people that you're leaving. A lot of folks have been awfully good to you. It's not fair to walk out of their lives without some sort of explanation. I'll have four cheeseburgers and two large orders of fries to go. And four of those apple pies, please," he said to the girl behind the counter and then turned back to me. "Like you did with the Caldwells."

"I've been busy," I mumbled.

"Heroes are allowed to have friends, too, you know," he said, running his hand over my brush cut. "Wait'll you see how many homeless children there are in Chicago. Why, a big city like that— there must be more than even you can take care of. I'll tell you what. Once we get settled, we'll look some of them up—see what we can do to help. I'll let you do all the talking, of course." He winked at me, and I blushed. "Thank you, Miss." He counted out some bills, and the girl gave him his change and two white bags.

"By the way," he said over his shoulder as we walked back through the restaurant, "you're wrong about me being like everybody else. I'll never be like everybody else again, and neither will you. And just for that you can carry these bags home."

He opened the door for me, and we started down the street. "I didn't mean . . ."

"Don't talk," he said. "Just carry the bags."

"Yes, sir."

TERRY

June 18, 1992

The next day Al was waiting for me like we'd planned. I walked past him so fast he had to run for a couple of seconds to catch up.

"Let's take the shortcut," I said without looking at him.

"But Mrs. Danbury doesn't like us cutting through her yard, remember?"

I started walking diagonally across Mrs. Danbury's lawn.

Al didn't say anything else for a while, which was a good thing since I had butterflies zapping my stomach and wasn't in the mood to talk.

When we got to the market parking lot, I picked out a big mini-van and pulled Al behind it. "This is it," I said. "Now we wait."

"What if he doesn't come to the market today?" Al asked.

I didn't answer. Part of me was hoping he *wouldn't* come. Al heaved a big sigh and squatted down to lean up against the van, and I started watching people load bags of groceries into their cars like it was something I'd never seen before. I was just wondering how long I'd stick it out before giving up when a huge shiny black limousine pulled up in front of the market. What was this? Somebody's maid being dropped off with a mile-long list and a wad of bills? A millionaire picking up some blueberry muffins for his breakfast? I slid to the front of the van and peeked over the hood to get a better look. "Now, *these* are rich people," I said.

Al's head poked up next to mine. "Hey, I know that car! It belongs to Mrs. Marsh! Mom told me she and her husband used to be the wealthiest people in the city before he died. He had that car made special with his family crest right up there on the front, you see it? Now the old lady just rides around in it by herself."

I whistled. "Must be worth a mint."

"Yeah. Mom says she still has a bundle and passes it around to all kinds of charities."

· The rear door of the limo opened, and what I saw next almost made me choke on my own spit. Below the door frame dropped a red canvas high-top sneaker—my hightop sneaker. It was Chive, all right, nodding and waving to the inside of that backseat like he did it every day.

"Do you see that?" squealed Al.

"Shhhh!" I said, pulling him down out of sight.

"What're you doing? I thought you wanted to talk to him."

"I do, but let's see what he does first."

Al peeked around the side of the van. "Well, you're not going to see him do anything. He's gone—and so's the limo."

"How could he be gone already?"

"Hey, did he ever say anything to you about being a magician?"

"Knock it off," I said. "Maybe he went in the store."

"Or maybe he got back in the limo and rode off into the sunset. The end."

Well, good for him, I thought. When you're home-hunting, you've got to keep at it until you find the best. A movement from the right side of the parking lot caught my eye, and Chive's head popped up over the top of this little red sports car like a jack-in-the-box. "Whoa—there he is!"

"Where?"

I pointed as Chive stood up and walked around the front of the car, his expression cool and serious. He looked like he'd just dropped a mask over his face—or taken one off. We followed his eyes and saw a woman pushing an overloaded shopping cart toward a bank of cars on the far side of the lot. He started walking smoothly through the car maze toward her. When he got within a few feet, this incredible change came over him. The coolness disappeared, and in its place was the bouncy, smiley kid I had first seen in this lot three months ago.

"Pardon me, ma'am," his voice chirped across the lot.

"There he goes," said Al. "Moving in for the kill." I sat down and leaned my head against the fender. "Boy, he's good at this—you should watch!"

"I've already seen it," I said.

I turned around in time to see Chive go into his head-shaking, hand-waving, no-ma'am-put-away-your-money routine. He waited until the woman drove out of sight and was checking the place out for another victim when the market door opened and a man in a long apron came out, flapping his arms and shouting. "Come on, kid—stop bothering the customers! I don't want to have to tell you again, you hear?" Chive laughed and backed around the corner of the store.

"Let's go!" I said, dragging Al from our hiding place.

We followed Chive at a distance, stopping and ducking behind buildings when we thought he might turn around. But he seemed pretty wrapped up in getting where he was going and didn't look right or left. We did, though. It didn't happen all at once, but the farther we walked, the rattier the neighborhood got. Dad would have a fit if he knew I was doing this.

"Now where's he going?" Al asked.

"How should I know?" Chive made a left, and I recognized the old section of town up ahead of us. "My great-uncle Bud used to live in one of these brownstones about fifty years ago."

"Really? I hope they looked better in those days than they do now."

"Yeah," I said, taking in the gutted heaps of crumbling brick and the boarded-up windows.

"Do you think people really live here?"

I looked up at the few windows that had curtains or a plant hanging in them. "I guess."

An old lady leaned out over our heads and yelled down to a little boy who was throwing chunks of plaster at a parked car. Other than that the street was deserted.

"This is Carter!" Al hissed in my ear and stopped.

"I know that!" I whispered back fiercely.

"It doesn't creep you out?"

"No!"

"Then why are you whispering?"

Everybody knew about Carter Street. It was the invisible line that divided our side of town from no-man's-land. Dad said anyone crossing Carter Street was looking for trouble. Well, I guessed that's what we were doing—looking for trouble.

"Are you coming?" I asked Al in a normal tone of voice. "He's getting away!"

Chive had turned right onto Buchanan and was trotting along like he was out for a stroll in the park.

We made the turn and continued our game of hide-and-seek.

"Watch it!" I steered Al around a drunk who was curled up on the sidewalk with his bottle.

"Yuck," said Al, holding his nose.

None of it bothered Chive, though. Up ahead of us he waved to three men standing outside a cigarette store. They gave him a nod and a "Hey" and went back to their talking. Al and I smiled shakily in their direction as we passed, but they didn't even look up. Then we saw it.

"Hey, that must be the Buchanan Arms," Al said. "What a scuzzy-looking place."

He had that right. It was hard to see how it had ever been the fancy hotel Dad said it was. One whole side was dark from smoke damage, and people were packed into it like sardines. They hung out of the windows; they called things to the women and children who were waiting in a line that went out the big front door and down the steps onto the sidewalk. It sounded like two or three different arguments were going on inside.

An official-looking woman came out and stood on the top step. "Please have all your papers ready when you get to the reception desk! If you don't have them with you, you'll have to go back to your office of origination to get them!" She went back inside the building, and a couple of the mothers in line started swearing.

Chive came alive and crossed the street. He

scooted along from garbage can to parked car until he was on the other side of the building.

"What's he doing? Did he see us?" I asked.

"Nah, he keeps looking at the Arms. Maybe he had a fight with someone in there," said Al.

"Mr. Nice Guy in a fight? Get real."

We hurried to catch up with him, then crept to the end of the next building and peeked around the corner. Chive was heading into a doorway halfway up the block.

"Here we go," I said, but Al's hand pulled me back so hard, I lost my balance and fell. "Wha—?" His eyes were almost bugging out of his head, and I turned to see what he was staring at.

Chive had never made it through the doorway. Instead, he was being pinned up against the building wall by two big kids wearing leather jackets and motorcycle boots.

"Where'd *they* come from?" I asked.

"I don't know. They must have been waiting for him. Terry, look—that guy's got a knife! And what's that thing the other one's waving around in the air?"

"A chain, I think."

The knife kid was doing most of the talking, and I could see Chive's eyes blink as spit sprayed his face.

"I don't like this," I said. "We've got to do something."

"Like what?" squeaked Al.

"Well, there're three of us and two of them."

"I thought you were mad at Chive."

"That doesn't mean I'm going to let him get beat up."

I thought I heard Al gulp.

The knife kid stepped to one side, still keeping a tight hold on Chive, and the other one started twirling his chain like he was winding up for a pitch.

"Now!" I shouted, bursting from our hiding place and hoping that Al was right behind me.

As if it were in slow motion, I saw the tip of the chain swing back and start its trip toward Chive's stomach. I was about three feet from the guy when I made my leap. I landed squarely on his back, my arms around his neck. We fell forward, and I heard the chain clatter to the ground. A grunting noise from the knife guy told me that Al had hit his mark too.

"The knife!" I yelled.

A red hightop sneaker swung past my face, and the knife went spinning across the street. Meanwhile I had my own problems. The chain kid had recovered from my surprise attack and was trying to roll over on top of me. I kept waiting for Al or Chive to pull him off, but it sounded like they were busy too. One good shove and my guy plopped himself down on my chest with his knees on either side of me. I was watching the fist he had aimed at my face and thinking, This is it, when he sud-

denly screamed "Aaagh" and made a grab for his
shoulder. I didn't know what had happened, but
I took the opportunity to slide out from under him
and get my bearings. There seemed to be more
than five of us now, and I was confused by the
sight of so many flying bodies.

To my right Chive and Al were still trying to tame
the knife guy. Al had him around the waist and
Chive was hanging on to one of his boots, but he
was much bigger than either of them, and they
were flopping around like fish. I crawled over to
help and was just about to grab the other boot
when pain shot through the back of my right knee.
"Ouch!" I yelled.

"No, Hatter! He's one of ours!" shouted Chive.

A little boy in a baseball cap took his teeth out
of my leg and crawled up alongside of me. While
Chive and I wrestled with the knife guy's feet, Al
threw himself at his head. Then, when we had
finally gotten him stretched facedown on the sidewalk, the little boy climbed onto the guy's butt and
started jumping up and down.

I glanced over to see what was happening with
the chain kid and was surprised to see P.B. and a
small dark-haired girl beating all over him with
their little fists. He was trying to catch them, but
they were too fast for him—one keeping up on the
beating while the other hopped out of his reach.
"Ow! Hey! Cut that out!"

"Okay!" I heard the knife guy say. His face was

pressed into the pavement, and his words came out muffled and jerky because of the bouncing kid on his backside. "Let—me—up!"

"Get the knife," Chive said. I ran across the street and picked the knife out of the gutter where it had landed while Al and Chive held down its owner. "All right, Hatter—that's enough." Chive reached up and helped the little boy step off his victim. "So, Pete—are you going to leave us alone now?" he asked the knife kid.

"You know this guy?" I asked.

"Sure, we're old friends—right, Pete?"

"Yeah," came the mumbled answer.

Chive nodded at Al, and they released their hold.

"Not too fast," I said, keeping the knife trained on him as he straightened.

Behind me the chain guy was still being punished. "Help! Oof! Get 'em off me!"

Chive jumped up. "Hey, kids! You can stop now! Good work!"

Out of the corner of my eye I saw the little girl get in one last punch.

"Why you . . . !" sputtered the kid.

He lunged at her, but Chive pushed his way between them. "Do you want me to sic them on you again?" he asked. The kid backed off.

"Gimme my knife," Pete said, holding his open hand out toward me and trying to look mean.

"I don't think so," I said.

Chive came over and took the knife from me.
"Like you said, Pete—my knife is so little. A big
one sure comes in handy every once in a while."
He smiled and then his voice turned dark and low.
"Now, get out of here."

We stood with the smaller kids gathered around
us until Pete and his buddy were out of sight. Then
the little girl burst into tears.

"Now, now, Missy." Chive sat down on the curb
and pulled her into a hug. "You were a brave girl,
you know that?"

"That was that bad boy again," Missy hiccuped.

"Yes, it was, but he won't be back. I think he's
scared of you!" Missy stopped crying and let Chive
work on her tear-stained face with the bottom of
his T-shirt. "That was a close one," Chive said over
the little ones' heads. "Thanks, you guys."

Al glanced over at me. "Yeah, well—we were in
the neighborhood."

I felt a poke in my side, and P.B. said, "I didn't
bite you, Terry. That was Hatter."

"Oh, yeah?" I leaned across P.B. and gave Hatter's baseball cap a swat. "You've got some sharp
teeth there."

"Thank you," Hatter said and grinned. "Are you
Terry? Where's the whistle Earl made you?"

I frowned. "Who's Earl?" I asked. And how did
this kid know who I was?

"Earl's my pop," Chive mumbled into Missy's
hair.

"You never told us you had a father," said Al.

He never told us he didn't, I thought. "And this must be your little sister, Missy," I said, putting the pieces together.

"No, silly!" Missy giggled into her hands. "I'm not Chive's sister!"

"Hey—you kids must be hungry," Chive said. "Why don't you go on in and make yourselves a snack."

"Can I have an Oreo?" asked Missy.

"I'm going to see if there's any more peanut butter left," said you-know-who.

"Can I have some peanut butter *on* an Oreo?" asked Hatter.

"Whatever you want," said Chive, shooing them through the doorway.

Of course. The guy I had seen in the bleachers at the tournament. But why the big secret? And who was Missy? Or was this all part of Chive's little game?

Chive caught me staring at him and plastered on a big smile. "Hey, how'd you guys find me? Boy, I've been so busy, I haven't had time to get over and see you all."

"So, where do you keep the limo parked?" I asked.

"Oh, you saw that. Um—she's just this lady I know."

"This *rich* lady you know," I said and tried to laugh.

"Yeah, we hear you know lots of people," Al added.

"How many kids have you got in there, anyway?" I asked.

Chive was starting to squirm, and I liked it. "Right now—just the ones you saw. They're friends of mine."

Like we're friends of yours? I wanted to ask. Al was right. They had a whole racket going on here.

"Where's your dad?" asked Al.

"Out on a construction job."

Oh, sure. He was probably the ringleader—out casing the area for families he and Chive could sucker.

"Did you spend all your prize money yet?" It was getting tougher to keep the hard edge out of my voice.

Chive licked his lips and hesitated. "Well, most of it went toward medicine for Missy. She's been sick. Like I told you."

"Yeah, I remember," I said through tight lips. "You also told us she was your sister."

"Well, yeah . . . "

"So, why'd you tell us that if it wasn't true? I mean, we don't care if you have a sister or not."

"Terry . . . " Al knew I was seconds away from totally losing it.

"You don't even have a sister, do you?"

"No! I mean, yes!"

I yelled down at him. "What other lies did you

tell us, huh? How about all the other people you stayed with—did you lie to them too?"

"I don't have a sister now, but I did have one!" Chive shouted back. "She was . . . she . . . " His face went all twisted, and I was about to yell at him again. Then it hit me. I had seen that look before. The night he had the nightmare. "I had a sister! I had a sister!" he kept screaming over and over.

"Sarry," I whispered, and the screaming stopped.

He looked up into my eyes for a long time and then crumpled forward until his forehead rested on his knees. His shoulders began to shake, and Al and I sat down on either side of him.

We let him cry for a while, taking turns patting his back. And when he could talk again, he told us. All about his mom and Sarry and the farm and everything that had happened to them since they lost it. I kept looking at him, trying to match up the person that had been through all that stuff with the kid who skateboarded up and down my driveway. It was like he was from a foreign country—one I never wanted to visit. I felt both lucky and stupid at the same time.

"Why didn't you tell us?" I asked when he had finished. "We wouldn't have told anybody." Al was still so weirded-out by Chive's story, he could only nod his head in agreement.

Chive squinted up into the sky, avoiding our faces. "I guess I thought if I told one person, I wouldn't be able to stop. That I'd forget and tell someone else, and then the welfare office would find out, and the kids would have to go back to the shelters and . . . "

I held my hand up to let him know I got the point. He sighed, and it was like watching a tight ball of string start to unwind from somewhere deep inside of him.

"I still don't know how you can live like this," Al said. "I almost fell over some drunk on the sidewalk back there. Hey, that wasn't your dad, was it?"

"No!" said Chive. He laughed and gave Al a shove.

"Al!" I said.

"Well, I didn't know!" Al said, his face getting red. "He could have been faking. You know, standing guard or something? Or *lying down* guard!" That made Chive laugh harder, and I joined him. Both of us started whacking at Al, who tried to duck away from our hands. "Stop it, you guys!"

"That wasn't him!" I said, giving Al one last swat on the back. "I saw him at the tournament. He looks just like Chive."

"You saw him?" Chive shook his head. "I told him not to come. But you know dads." It was good to see him smile again.

"Yeah. So, where is he now?"

"Working—really. He goes around to different construction sites outside the city. But not for long!

He's just finishing up on this one job before we move to Chicago. The last thing he said to me before he left was, 'Now, Son, you'd better start getting yourself all packed up and ready to go.' Like I really have anything to pack!"

Chicago!

"You're moving?" asked Al.

"Yep—in two weeks! The company Pop's going to work for is fixing us up with an apartment, and they're going to lend him a car until we can afford one for ourselves. Pop even thinks they might promote him to supervisor in a couple months."

"Hey, that's cool," I said, trying to mean it.

He looked away, embarrassed. "Well, it's good for me and Pop, I guess." He licked one finger and started rubbing at a dirty spot on his sneakers. Then he must have remembered that they used to be mine, because he stopped. "But I don't know what's going to happen to the kids. They're used to having me around, and this place isn't safe anymore. . . ."

"That's okay! You just go on to Chicago! We can take care of ourselves just fine without you!"

We turned toward the dark doorway, and P.B. stepped out into the sunlight. His eyes were bright and angry.

"How long have you been standing there, huh?" asked Chive. "Come here." He held out his hand, but P.B. pretended not to see it.

"How far away is Chicago, anyway? Maybe I'll

go with you. Make some new friends. I'm tired of this dopey old place."

Chive went and knelt down so he was eye to eye with him. "Now, you know you can't do that. What would Linda say?"

"She wouldn't mind."

I thought I saw Chive wince and realized that P.B. was probably right about his mother not missing him if he were gone. Chive looked at Al and me, and that's when I knew I didn't have any other choice.

I stood up and said, "But, P.B., you've got to stay here with us. You know all the other kids, right?"

P.B. nodded stiffly but kept his eyes on Chive.

"Well, after Chive goes, we're going to need someone to help us keep track of them and find them places to stay."

"And you probably know a lot of the families they stayed with too," added Al.

"Sure," said P.B., looking at us out of the corner of one eye. "There's the Lopnows. And the Praegers. The Frascottis, your house, Mrs. Marsh, Mrs. Conte, the Warn—"

"Okay," I said. "We don't need them all right now, but we're going to. You're going to have to introduce us to everybody. It's a big job."

"I can handle it," P.B. said.

Chive stood and faced me. "Terry, you don't have to do this," he said in a low voice. "These kids got by before I butted into their lives—they'll manage somehow. At least that's what Pop keeps telling me."

"No, I'm going to do it," I said, but I felt a little dizzy and had to sit down on the curb again. "How many kids are there *really?*"

P.B. must have decided this was part of his new job, because he sat down next to me and started singing, "There's Missy and Socks and Hatter and Froggie and—"

"Froggie!" said Al.

Chive giggled. "Wait'll you hear him talk."

Al shook his head. "You guys have the weirdest names."

"Oh, they're not real. We used nicknames so no one could connect us to our welfare records."

"Wait a minute—you mean, like Missy for Maria, right?" I asked.

"Yeah," said Chive, frowning. "How'd you know that?"

"Uh . . ." I wasn't ready to let Chive in on my career as a spy yet. "I'll tell you later," I mumbled.

"So then, what's *your* real name?" asked Al.

"Charles. Charles Horton."

Al screwed up his face. "I'd stick to Chive if I were you."

"So, how many?" I asked again.

"It depends." Chive sat on the curb to my left, and Al sat on the other side of P.B. "I've had as many as nine in the hideout at one time. They come and go. Sometimes I won't see some kids for weeks at a time, and then all of sudden every momma in town needs to drop off her kid for a few days. Of course, most of the time I try to park them for the night with a nice family like—" He stopped and turned red. "Well, you know. . . ."

"Yeah, we know," said Al and laughed.

"Do you think these families will still want to help with the kids after you're gone?" I asked, trying not to sound as nervous as I felt.

Chive snorted. "You sure weren't too happy when you found out I was staying all over the place. I'd be afraid to ask them."

All four of us stared out into the street for a few seconds. "Well, I wouldn't!" said Al. He jumped up and brushed off the seat of his jeans. "The first thing we've got to do is talk to every kid at school who's had someone stay with them."

"Good idea," I said.

"We've got six more school days left. We'll let everybody know what the deal is and find out how many families we can count on."

"Yeah," I said, "my mom can make phone calls to all her friends. She loves this kind of stuff." I was feeling better already.

"I hope I can reach all the kids and their folks before I leave." Chive shook his head. "I still worry about someone coming to the hideout and finding no one here."

I patted Chive's shoulder. "Like Al said—we'll

be out of school soon. We can take turns keeping watch in case anyone shows up."

"Or I can leave a note upstairs," Chive said. "You guys shouldn't be hanging around a neighborhood like this."

Al looked hurt. "Are you saying we can't take care of ourselves? Didn't you see us back there against Pete and company? We were bad! How do you think I'd look in one of those leather jackets?"

"Like you were out trick-or-treating," I said. "Anyway, it's all settled; we can work out the details later. What time is it?"

Al looked at his watch. "Almost five-thirty. No wonder I'm hungry."

"We'd better get home. Chive, do you want to come over to my house for dinner?"

Chive shook his head. "No, I'd better stay here and tell the kids what's happening. I've got to do it sometime."

"Well, we'll be back tomorrow. We've got a ton of stuff to do."

"I'll come over some other night, though— maybe bring Pop along, too, if that's all right. I want to say good-bye to your folks and Louanne."

"Or you can take her with you to Chicago," I said.

Chive smiled, but his eyes looked sad.

"How come Louanne can go and I can't?" whined P.B.

"She can't," I said. "I was just kidding."

"Oh," said P.B. "Well, maybe I should go home with you now and tell her about Chive. I'm real good with little kids."

We all laughed. "That's a good idea, P.B.," I said. "Then, let's get going. Do you have a sweater or something for later?"

"Why don't you take my Triple Threat jacket?" said Chive. "It's yours now."

P.B.'s eyes opened wide. "You mean it? I can keep it? Wait right here," he ordered us and ran through the doorway. We could hear him taking the stairs two at a time.

I could see the gears grinding away in Chive's head, and I asked the question with my eyes. "Oh, I'm just thinking," he said. "You're going to have to keep an eye on Socks. He looked kind of banged up the last time his mom dropped him off."

I nodded.

"Also, make sure Bucky gets something to eat when you see him. He's real skinny."

"Okay."

"Oh, and don't let your mom put too much fertilizer on that plum tree of hers—"

"Hey!" I said. "You're awful bossy for someone who's not even going to be around."

Chive smiled and shut up.

"Okay, I'm ready!" said P.B., popping into the street. He was trying to roll up the sleeves of Chive's jacket so he could find his hands.

"I don't think you need that on," Al said. "It's still pretty warm out."

"I was a little chilly," P.B. said, ignoring the drop of sweat that ran down the side of his head. "Chive, after you move to Chicago, will you come back and visit us?"

"Yes, I'll come back and visit," he said, and he looked directly at me. "I promise."

Satisfied with Chive's answer, P.B. wedged himself between Al and me and took one of our hands in each of his.

"See you tomorrow," I said to Chive.

"Hey, Ter, do we have a social studies test tomorrow?" asked Al.

"Yeah. Have you studied for it?"

"Nope. Just you wait, Horton. Before you know it, you'll be taking tests like the rest of us."

Chive rolled his eyes and waved as the three of us started down the street. When I moved my left leg, I could feel a lump swelling from where the chain guy and I had hit the ground. I was tired, too, but I couldn't stop the thoughts that kept whirling around in my head.

"Do you think people will listen to us?" I asked Al.

"I don't know. It's worth a try. I can't believe how many kids he's been looking after."

"Tell me about it." I was used to worrying about one homeless kid. Now I realized they were everywhere.

P.B. tugged at our hands again. "Now that I'm a

Triple Threat, I'm going to need my own skateboard.
Do you think Chive'll take his board with him?"

"Who said you were going to be in the Threats?"
asked Al.

"I know all the moves! And I've got some new
ideas, wait'll you hear!"

"Yeah, I'll bet," said Al.

P.B. dragged down on our arms. "Pleeease."

"We'll see," I said, smiling over at Al.

"Listen to this! How about a three-man jump
from the ramp? Wouldn't that be cool?" He did a little
hop to demonstrate.

"Cool." I couldn't look Al straight in the eye.

"Or a figure eight. Get it? One guy starts to make
a loop, like this." He stepped out in front of us and
leaned to the left. "Then when he gets to the top of
the loop, he leans to the right, and the second guy
starts out and does the same thing." He scooted back,
nearly tripping us. "Now the third guy leans to the
left, and the first guy is at the bottom of the loop,
leaning to the right. . . ."

"Remind me to kill Chive before he leaves town,"
Al said, and I burst out laughing.

P.B. stopped his zigzagging and looked back at us.
"What's so funny?" he asked.

EPILOGUE

The Citizens Gazette,
June 7, 1993

SKATEBOARD TOURNAMENT
BENEFITS HOMELESS

A record 2000 people were on hand for the Perkins County Skateboard Tournament, held this past Saturday, June 5, in the Morrison Junior High School parking lot. An annual event since 1987, this year's tournament was dedicated to more than the fun of skateboarding. For several weeks Perkins County elementary and junior high school students have been writing and distributing press releases to local newspapers and radio and television stations, announcing that all proceeds from the tournament would be donated to the Chive Garden Home for Children.

The Chive Garden, converted from the home and estate of philanthropist Mrs. Cyril Marsh, opened its doors last September in response to a growing need for temporary housing and care for our city's homeless children. Project Chairman Mrs. Philip Caldwell told us in a recent phone conversation that the Garden is currently operating at full capacity, and a long waiting list has been established. "I am delighted that so many students seem to be taking an active interest in the Garden. I only hope that more people will come forward to help by making donations or providing temporary shelter for a homeless child."

Spectators at Saturday's tournament were treated to a wide variety of skateboarding expertise. Allen Drucker won first prize in the solo event, and despite the presence of several three-man teams in this year's multiple-board competition, none was a match for the daring of the Fearless Four on Wheels. The high point of the Fearless Four's routine was their final jump, in which they joined hands and executed a four-man takeoff from a raised platform. When asked later how they came up with such an unusual move, the team's smallest member took full credit for the idea.

About the Author

Shelley A. Barre was born in Buffalo, New York. A graduate of Denison University, she spent several years acting on Broadway and performing in her own rock band. She now teaches classes and seminars for both adults and children in creative writing. She has had articles published in *Glamour* magazine and *The New York Times*. This is her first novel.

Ms. Barre and her husband divide their time between Peekskill, New York, and the Catskill Mountains.